Lucky

Rise of the Pride

Book 13

Theresa Hissong

All rights reserved. This book or parts thereof may not be reproduced in any form, stored in any retrieval system, or transmitted in any form by any means—electronic, mechanical, photocopy, recording, or otherwise—without prior written permission of the publisher, except as provided by United States of America copyright law.

2022 Theresa Hissong
All Rights Reserved

Disclaimer:
This book is a work of fiction. Any resemblance to any person, living or dead is purely coincidental. The names of people, places, and/or things are all created from the author's mind and are only used for entertainment.

Due to the content, this book is recommended for adults 18 years and older.

Cover Design:
Gray Publishing Services

Editing by:
Heidi Ryan
Amour the Line Editing

Formatted by:
Imagine Ink Designs

For more information or how to contact Theresa Hissong, please visit:

http://authortheresahissong.com
www.facebook.com/authortheresahissong

Table of Contents

Prologue...1
Chapter 1..3
Chapter 2..13
Chapter 3..29
Chapter 4..39
Chapter 5..53
Chapter 6..63
Chapter 7..73
Chapter 8..85
Chapter 9..93
Chapter 10...103
Chapter 11...117
Chapter 12...135
Chapter 13...145
Chapter 14...153
Chapter 15...165

Dedication:

This one is for those few who've fallen in love at first sight.

Prologue

10 Years Ago...

It was time to fight for his spot as a Guardian, but his recent maturity had changed his life and way of thinking. There was a yearning inside him that made Lucky Cooper want more...a lot more. His father had told him of the time he would find his mate, and that conversation spiraled into his new life as a Guardian once he won his position with Talon's men.

The moment he came out of the circle, bloody and bruised, he knew things would change, but what he didn't realize was that his true mate would eventually show herself many years later.

In his stubborn, and younger mind, he always wanted to immediately touch her to make the connection.

Oh, but things didn't always work out as they seemed.

The mating of a female was going to be more difficult than he ever thought.

He would have to wait for her.

When, and if, she was ever ready…

Chapter 1

"*You promised me you wouldn't* make a big deal about my birthday," Sofia grumbled to Savage the morning she turned twenty-three. He'd stopped by the tiny cabin that had been gifted to her by Malaki…her friend.

It still crushed her to know he'd left for nine months, only to return to see the alpha for a meeting, then leave again. It'd been two months since the last time she had seen him.

There was also the confusion on the day he returned. Sofia had not imagined a mating scent in the room when both Lucky and Malaki were there. And she hadn't scented it since.

"Well, I brought you gifts," her big ass brother admitted with a slight smirk at the corner of his mouth.

It wasn't a gesture many others saw. He kept that for his mate, Mary Grace, their mother, and Sofia. Even though her brother was one of the best Guardians, and sometimes quite the asshole, he had a soft spot for the women in his life.

"I don't like gifts," she reminded him.

"Okay," he chuckled in defeat with his hands raised in the air. "It's not really a gift…it's firewood. The weather is going to change in the next few nights, and they're calling for single digits and snow. I brought you some of mine until Storm and Lucky get another load split."

She didn't even flinch at the sound of Lucky's name coming from her brother. She'd become too numb to her feelings toward the male. There was something about him that piqued her interest, and her panther wasn't much help. The animal noticed him, but not in the way Sofia's human half did.

"I'm so glad I took this week off work for my vacation," she admitted when Savage returned from a short trip to her front porch. "I love the snow, but I hate driving in it." She shivered just from the thought of maneuvering down the slick, backcountry roads.

"I would've taken you into work," he grunted as he leaned over with a huge bundle of wood to set next to the small fireplace in her living room. There was an oval wood holder just off the side of the fireplace, and he took his time filling it up for her. Savage glanced at her a few times, but she tried to ignore it.

Lucky

Sofia knew her big brother wanted to ask about Malaki, and Lucky for that matter, but she wasn't going to get into a conversation with him about the two males. As far as she was concerned, the last two months were enough time to live her life. Worrying about those two males would've driven her crazy if she'd let it get to her.

Savage was notorious for being hard on Malaki when he had lived there and was in charge of security at her work during the time the wolves had been running feral. Lucky wasn't as scared of Savage as most of the younger Guardians. Her brother was known for his name, and he put fear into the younger ones' eyes with just one look, but Lucky was quickly becoming just as strong.

She didn't know much about what had been going on with Lucky in the last two months, because she had avoided him since Malaki had come and left again. It was probably for the best that Malaki was gone because she was tired of seeing her brother being an ass toward him. Hell, she was tired of everyone watching her friend, waiting for him to snap.

It's not like Malaki had no reasons for his attitude, either. He'd been through the unthinkable. Sofia pinched her eyes closed and held off on the tears as Savage finished stocking the wood for her stove.

The last thing she wanted to do was discuss her issues with her brother. Gods, he'd go feral himself. No one was good enough for her, and he'd been glaring at all of the males her age since she was fourteen. She held back a chuckle at remembering how mean he was to them.

She'd learned a long time ago to keep Savage out of her love life. It wasn't going to be good for anyone involved. Sofia was more of the *"If I tell him my problems, he's going to just beat someone until my problems go away. So, it's better to keep quiet,"* type. As much as she loved Savage, she needed to take care of her problems in her own way. Maiming them didn't do much good.

"I'll come by and shovel any snow that drifts up onto your porch," he stated as he set the last log onto the rack. "Don't try and walk out on it until I get the area cleared. You could fall."

She wasn't going to argue with him. So, instead, she stood as tall as she could and used one hand to tug on his collar so he'd lean down. With a soft peck to his cheek, she let go with a whispered word of thanks.

"Enjoy your time off," he said as he headed for the door. "I think Mary Grace is cooking a big dinner tonight. You know you're always welcome. Mom and Dad will be there, too."

"I do, and I may take you up on that offer," she agreed with a genuine smile. "Have her call me and let me know what to bring."

Savage left her there alone, and the small cabin grew quite of voices, but the pop and sizzle of the wood stove kept her thoughts from being cast into nothingness.

It was five days into the new year, and thankfully,

the human-animal clinic where she worked had decided to open only for emergencies because of the upcoming snowstorm. Everyone was given the choice of taking their vacation time or coming in on an as needed basis. Sofia wanted some time off. So, she was free to do as she pleased for the next seven days.

One glance out the large living room window and she knew it had been her best decision because snowflakes the size of quarters were beginning to fall. Several small panthers ran out into the woods, playing and having the times of their lives as their parents followed them down the trails. If everyone was this excited about the snow when it began to fall, she could only imagine what the cubs of the pride will be like in a few days when the ground was covered in the white stuff.

Talon and Liberty were right behind their two children, Ember and Declan, running into the forest behind the alpha's home. She longed to join them, but decided to head over to her brother's house instead after a quick text to his mate.

As soon as she arrived, her niece and nephew, Maya and Landon, came running into her awaiting arms. She'd always dreamed of having cubs of her own, but she had time because she was only twenty-three. There was plenty of time left in her life to find her true mate and start a family, and she wanted a large family if the gods graced her with one. She'd been through two of her annual fertile times, and she knew another one would be coming around the spring solstice. She didn't want to have to be sedated again, but it was inevitable. Without a mate to give you his seed for a cub, the need to mate was painful…and long. Last year, Harold had to sedate her for five days. It really sucked being a female.

"Auntie Sofia!" the cubs cheered as she set the potato salad on the table. "Come play with us." The oldest child, Landon, grabbed her hand and pulled her over to a set of building blocks. It was natural for him to take interest in the same thing his father did for a living when he wasn't protecting the pride.

"Are you going to build homes like your father?" She ruffled his dark brown hair when he smiled brightly and looked up at her with icy blue eyes. She'd seen pictures of Savage when he was seven, and Sofia swore they couldn't be told apart. Her niece, Maya, looked just like what she imagined Mary Grace as a child looked like.

Maya was toddling over to the building blocks, and Landon made room for his baby sister to sit next to him. Just like Savage had done with Sofia at an early age, Landon pulled his sister to his side and started showing her the basics of building a block house.

"He's very protective," Sofia mentioned as she left the two children to play.

"He's going to make for a fierce Guardian someday," Savage boasted with his chest puffed out like a proud father.

It wasn't long before their parents arrived, grabbing

Lucky

the children and playing with them as if they hadn't seen them in months. Sofia laughed because Savage's cubs were wrapped around her mom and dad's little fingers. She hoped one day she would have her own cubs to be loved by her family, as well.

Her mind wanted to wander to Malaki and Lucky, but she didn't let that happen. Instead, she busied herself helping Mary Grace with setting the table and gathering everyone for their dinner.

After everyone was fed, she cleaned the dishes and made small talk with her sister-in-law. She knew Mary Grace wanted to ask about the men in her life, but she kept it to herself. In all honesty, Sofia wanted to talk to someone, and she finally blurted out what was bothering her.

"Hey, look…" She paused to take a deep breath. After looking over her shoulder and seeing that Savage was deep in conversation with their father, she lowered her voice. "I need to talk to you, but…you know…my brother's hearing is really good."

"If it's about girl problems," Mary Grace winked, "I can walk you home after we finish."

"I'd appreciate that," she sighed.

They hurried along with the dishes, and once they were done, Mary Grace spoke up and narrowed her eyes at her mate, "I'm going to walk Sofia home."

"I can do that," Savage offered as he began to stand, but when his eyes caught the look on Mary Grace's face, he sat back down.

"We need some female time," his mate mumbled, knowing her brother would probably be weirded out by any talk of girl stuff. Sofia held back a chuckle at the way Savage shivered slightly. Of course, her parents were too busy to notice, because they were playing with the cubs.

After a round of goodbyes and a promise to Savage that Mary Grace would be home in a few minutes, the two of them headed out of the cabin and began their trek through the fresh snow. The only cabin across the alpha's expansive backyard was hers…well, Malaki's, and they'd promised they'd go there and nowhere else.

"Your brother is so fucking protective," Mary Grace laughed. Sofia chimed in and they bumped shoulders because they both knew how Savage was about his family.

"He will understand…maybe," Sofia laughed, and it felt good.

The moon was covered with thick clouds and snow was falling, but it'd slowed down since the sunset a few hours before. The crunch of the two women's boots echoed off the trees leading into the woods to their left.

"So, male trouble, huh?" Mary Grace finally asked.

"Um," Sofia scoffed. "Yeah."

"Which one is it?" she pressed.

"Both."

Mary Grace made a humming sound but didn't reply. It was driving Sofia crazy because she wanted advice. "Why are you so quiet?"

"Well, you tell me what you think," Mary Grace

pressed. "Then, I'll give my input."

"Ah, thanks a lot." Sofia rolled her eyes as she climbed the snowy steps to her cabin.

Once they were inside, she added a log to the wood stove and motioned for Mary Grace to take a seat on the couch. Once they were settled, Sofia covered her face with her hands and told her everything.

"I miss him…Malaki," she sighed. "I also enjoy my time with Lucky, but he's been distant since Mal left again. I'm confused. I know one of them is probably my mate because when Mal came home, I scented a mating scent that had to come from one of the two males, but I don't know which one. Ever since then, I haven't scented it again. Even when Malaki came to say goodbye after talking to Talon that night, nor when I've seen Lucky at the alpha's home…which has only been two times in the last two months."

"Mating scents don't always appear and stay there, Sofia," Mary Grace reminded her. "There's no way to know who it came from sometimes. Hell, there are plenty of times when the mating scents don't even show up until after a pair touches for the first time."

"You're not helping," Sofia frowned.

"I'm just being honest," she shrugged. Sofia held back tears when Mary Grace reached over and touched her hand. She knew what was coming next. "You know Malaki's not coming back, right?"

"I know," she sniffled and let the first tear fall.

Chapter 2

*L*ucky Cooper *stacked wood on* a trailer as he and his brother, Storm, worked for the last two days in the freezing temperatures to prepare enough firewood for the pride to heat their cabins for the next three or four days.

He'd never seen so much snow in his twenty-seven years of life, and the human news had warned it would stick to the ground until the temperatures warmed up later in the week.

He was bothered that Sofia was alone in her cabin more than he was worried for anyone else. Storm hadn't said anything to him since the night Malaki had shown up at the pride to speak with Talon and everyone in the house had noticed a mating scent in the air.

No one knew who it belonged to, either.

Except Lucky.

It was his, and he fucking knew it, but from that day on…it just disappeared. Of course, he'd wondered why, and then he wondered why it never happened again after Malaki returned to Louisiana where he was working with another pride to stop the drug trade and a rogue wolf pack that still plagued the area.

"Keep splitting that wood into shards, and no one will have a decent piece to keep them warm for longer than twenty minutes." Storm's voice broke through his thoughts. When Lucky looked down at the pile around him, he finally realized he'd stopped loading wood and started taking his frustrations out on a fresh set of logs that needed to be broken down.

"Fuck," he groaned. "Sorry."

He carefully set the ax next to the unsplit pile and began cleaning up his mess, but his brother's large feet came into view as he was bent over. "I don't want to talk about it, Storm."

"You need to," his brother warned, taking his foot and stepping on a log Lucky was trying to move. "I've never seen you this miserable."

"I am miserable," he huffed and stood upright. "It's cold, and I would like to get this done so I can relax until my shift tomorrow morning."

Storm paused and took a deep breath, narrowing his eyes as if he could see into Lucky's mind. Good thing he couldn't, because it wasn't a great place to be in at the moment.

Lucky

"Okay, you're my brother, and I know you, Lucky." Storm groaned, picking up a split log and tossing it in his direction. "Let's finish loading, and while we do, we will talk."

"I'm not talking," he began, but Storm wasn't having it. Lucky let out an "*oof*" when a log jammed into his stomach.

"Sofia is your mate, and you fucking know it," Storm advised, pointing toward the trailer. "Load and listen."

"Fine!" Lucky barked but did as he was told. "I guess we are doing this."

"So, your mating scent appeared when Malaki was here, but since then, you haven't had any reaction to the female, right?" Storm was the only other person who knew the truth about the night Malaki had showed up at the pride house.

"Oh, I've had a reaction, but it has nothing to do with my scent," he admitted. He'd dreamed about her for months, and every fucking morning, he'd woken with his hand around his cock as her name fell from his lips.

"What about Sofia?" Storm's voice was full of frustration, but Lucky wanted to just move on from the conversation. He knew his older brother wouldn't let up until they talked, and he gritted his teeth when he replied.

"What about her?" he asked, feeling his panther prowl under his skin. Yes, they were both protective of her.

"Her mating scent, dumbass," Storm huffed and

rolled his eyes. "Does she give off a scent when you two are together?"

"I wouldn't know." He shrugged and tossed another piece of wood on the trailer. "I've tried to give her some space. It's obvious she has feelings for Malaki, and I don't like him. It's probably for the best if we stay friends and don't get involved."

"You are the biggest idiot I've ever known, Lucky Cooper. Jesus, I know mom dropped you on your head when you were a cub. I remember it."

"Man, shut the fuck up," Lucky snarled, flashing his canines.

"Did you even wish her a happy birthday?" Storm pressed with the questions.

"Like I said," Lucky growled, but internally kicked himself for forgetting her birthday. "Shut the fuck up."

"Watch it, now," his older brother warned with a flash of amber eyes.

"Whatever," Lucky mumbled as he rolled his eyes when Storm wasn't looking. He didn't need an ass-kicking today, or the next, from his brother. Everyone knew Storm had become stronger since he'd mated Amaya. That female had changed him.

"I remember you telling me what a dumbass I was for not touching my mate," Storm reminded him. "You're doing the exact same thing."

Lucky stacked the wood on the trailer with nothing more than a grunt until the thing was overflowing. Storm shucked his gloves and climbed into the driver's seat of the old, white farm truck, and started his route heading to the furthest house away from the alpha's home.

Kye met them outside and helped with his own wood, shaking their hands before the two males left to hit the other cabins down the gravel road covered in snow. It was a slow process, but by the time they reached Sofia's, she was standing on the porch looking like a princess, bundled up in a long winter coat with fur around the neck.

"We brought you some firewood," Storm announced since Lucky couldn't think of anything to say to her. His panther was prowling in his mind, knowing she was living in Malaki's old home.

"Savage brought me some last night, but I could always use a little more," she said, pointing to a spot on the edge of the porch where Malaki had built a wall to cover his wood supply from the elements. Her stack was only half full, and that just wouldn't do.

"I have enough to fill that up for you," Lucky finally spoke as he caught her eyes. Tiny specks of amber were flickering in her icy blue stare. There was a heat in them he'd never noticed before.

And a sweet scent that instantly made his cock rock fucking hard.

"Unload," Storm barked. "I'm going to drop the trailer here and I'll come back later. She will need more than this." At that point, he ignored his brother and stood there watching her. After the roar of the truck's engine jarred him from his thoughts, he grabbed an armful of wood.

"Go inside, princess," he ordered. "It's too cold out here."

He wanted to hit himself with a log for slipping in the endearment he'd only used in his mind, but she didn't comment and did as he'd asked of her. Only to return a few moments later with a steaming mug, setting it down on the railing on her porch.

"I just made some hot cocoa," she announced. Her voice was so sweet and innocent, and it killed him to know that they were most likely mates. He wasn't the good guy or the sweet innocent baby brother to Storm Cooper. No, Lucky was too rough and crass for the likes of someone like Sofia Corvera, but her beauty made him want to be soft with her. "You look like you're freezing. Please, drink that so I know you're warm."

"Thank you." He nodded and picked up the cup. He moaned softly when the warm liquid hit his tongue. "This is good."

"My mother is an expert and taught me all the ways of making a good cup of hot chocolate." The giggle died on her lips when he looked up over the rim of the cup.

Over the chocolate and the wood, their mating scents thickened in the cold air. She scented him while he was already inhaling her sweet smell regardless of the drink. Gods, she smelled like cotton candy and home.

"Happy birthday, by the way," he blurted, taking another sip of the delicious liquid.

"Thank you." She blushed.

Lucky

There was no sound between them for a few heartbeats as their scents mingled in the cold night air. The flutter of snowflakes was nothing more than soft background music.

"Lucky?" she whispered...shocked. Her own cup slipped from her hand, but she quickly righted herself and set it down. "It was you?"

"Yeah," he said, setting the cup down beside hers. One touch and everything would change. She wouldn't have a choice, and most males didn't ever take that from their females. Lucky grew up with integrity, and his father and brother both told him it was more respectful for him to let his female make the initial touch once he'd found her. It was just the way he had been raised, but fuck if he didn't want to just take her into his arms at that moment. The only thing holding him back was where they were at...Malaki's old cabin.

He wasn't sure what happened between Storm and Amaya, or how their mating went down, and to be honest, he didn't want to know. He just knew things were tense with them for a long time. Everyone was different. Some males had told the others about it, but others kept their mating nights private. He surely didn't want any details about his brother's first night with his mate, but he could use a little guidance at the moment.

"Why didn't you tell me?" she growled, wrapping her long coat tighter around her body and taking a step toward him. He couldn't move away because his back was to the wall of firewood.

"Don't come any closer, Sofia," he warned with a flash of his canines. "There's a lot I have to consider about my feelings for you."

"You have feelings for me? Really?" she barked. Her eyes immediately glowed amber. Her panther was on edge, and his first reaction was to comfort her, but he held it back. "After Mal showed up, you ghosted me! I haven't seen you at all, Lucky. Why? Tell me why?"

"That's my business," he barked.

"I deserve to know!" she hollered. Now, the female was angry…very angry. He'd never seen her like that before, and he didn't like it. Not. One. Bit. "One of you had a mating scent that day at the alpha's home, and I've been losing my mind wondering who it belonged to, and you knew it all along."

"You have feelings for *him*," Lucky growled. He couldn't even say the male's name out loud. Malaki had caused so much trouble since he had turned twenty and went through his human equivalent of puberty in their world. The male's hatred for everything made it hard to work with him or even hold a conversation.

He'd changed even more when Taze and Malaki's sister, Calla, mated. There was so much resentment and history due to their time as pawns for the wolves. Lucky wasn't sure there was any hope to help Malaki, but for some reason, he was gentle with Sofia. No one understood why, either.

"He's my *friend*, Lucky," she sighed, rubbing her temples like she had a headache. "That's it. There's nothing between us, and I promise you we've never touched. He's respectful toward me, and we actually get along. Everyone hates him, but they just don't understand him."

"We don't hate him." Well, Lucky did because the male was so close to Sofia.

"That's a lie, and you know it," she accused, tucking her winter coat tighter around her small body after she'd let it go to point a finger in his direction. "He's been through some terrible things, and he's trying to work through them. Now, he's gone…probably forever. Everyone around here avoids him because he isn't like the rest of the Guardians."

"No, we avoid him because he is an asshole," Lucky admitted, pausing when she glared at him.

"Well, he wasn't like that with me," she reminded him.

"I think we should not be around each other for a while," Lucky suggested. "I know you're not ready to explore this mating scent, and to be honest, I don't think I am either, knowing you might have feelings for Malaki more than you believe you do."

"Fine," she barked, turning on her heel. The mating scent was gone, and Lucky felt like someone had punched him in the gut. He started to walk off the porch when she turned around with tears in her amber eyes. "All I've ever wanted was for everyone to get along, but I can see that will never happen."

Lucky left her alone as she'd asked, but she didn't want him to leave. Neither did her panther. Sofia finally knew who had been giving off the mating scent that day two months ago, but she was so damn mad at everyone for the way they treated Malaki the last time he was at the pride. She was bitter.

All she wanted to do was to talk to him, but he hadn't answered his phone when she had called him over the last two months. Just like he refused her calls during the nine months he was gone before that.

She sat in the dark brown recliner that belonged to him and held her phone tightly. Should she try again? Would he answer? What would she say? There was no way she could tell him she found her true mate in one of the Guardians that hated him.

Without a second thought, the phone was to her ear, and with each unanswered ring, a tear would roll down her cheek. When his voicemail picked up, she whispered into the phone, "I miss you, Mal. Please, come home."

She dropped the phone on the end table and stared out the window, seeing as another day was ending and night would be upon the pride in moments. The snow was falling harder, and she tried to find excitement in knowing the morning would bring with it several more inches, but she couldn't bring herself to feel anything other than loss.

She leaned back in the recliner and closed her eyes.

Lucky

When she opened them again, it was early morning, and just as the weatherman had predicted, there was an abundance of snow covering everything. She stretched and wrapped the blanket she kept on the chair around her body while fumbling with a few logs of wood to add to the dying fire. The cabin was cold, but she called upon her panther, shifting slightly to use her animal for warmth until the wood fire could heat her little home.

When she approached the front window, she frowned. It looked like Savage had already come by and swept off her porch. There wasn't a speck of snow on the steps, either. Smiling to herself, she walked over to the little kitchen and started a cup of coffee. There was a book laying on the counter she'd planned on reading the night before but hadn't because she had fallen asleep in the chair.

Tucking it under her arm, she held her coffee with both hands as she turned for the little two-seater table in the corner of the room. She'd get lost in the book for the day since it was technically her vacation.

Sounds of footsteps coming to her door made her pause. She knew it was her brother from the heavy steps he took. "Come in, Savage!"

"Morning," he grumbled, narrowing his eyes at her.

"What?" she replied and stood.

"I told you I'd sweep off your porch this morning," he reminded her. "You didn't have to do it."

"I didn't," she frowned, confused. "It was like that when I woke up."

She didn't remember hearing anyone come or go, but then again, she had been passed out cold in the recliner.

"Then who came by?"

"I have an idea," she mumbled and changed the subject. It had to have been Lucky. "Want some coffee?"

"I heard you," he huffed. "Was it Lucky or Malaki?"

"Malaki? Why would you even ask me that, Savage? You know he's not here!" The audacity of her brother to bring up Mal's name when he already knew she struggled with him being gone.

"Because he came home last night," he announced, taking a step toward her when she swayed.

All of the blood fled her brain, and she did sway. Fucking hell! "He's…he's here?"

"He made it to the pride around two this morning," Savage informed her. Sofia felt her heart swell, knowing he was there. "He's in a meeting with Talon, and I want you to stay away from him for the day."

"You can't order me to stay away from him, Savage," she snarled, feeling her panther rush to the surface. "I live in his cabin!"

"He doesn't want the cabin." Savage shook his head and covered a yawn behind his hand. "He's staying in the old dorms for now."

"Wait," she paused, noticing that her brother had gone without sleep, "have you been awake since he got here?"

"I can't go into details with you, and you know that.

It's Guardian business." Savage's word was final, and everyone knew the Guardians had a very tight honor system when it came to anything business related to the pride and their safety.

"I don't give a fuck about Guardian business, Savage." She bared her fangs at him. "I'm going to see him."

"Not today," Savage warned and his eyes flashed amber. "Stay away from Malaki. Give him time to adjust being back,"

"Adjust?" she gasped, placing her hand over her rapid heart. "He's taken Talon's blood again?"

Savage didn't answer, but his canines lengthened.

"Damn it, Savage! Answer me!" Oh, she was so angry. She was an adult female and could make decisions on her own, but her brother was a beast and lived by his given name twenty-four-freaking-seven!

"He just got back from his shift and is resting," Savage finally said. "Give him some time to sleep from the drive up from New Orleans."

"Fine," she huffed. "But just remember that I *will* be seeing him tonight. I have to talk to him one on one."

"Don't touch him," Savage warned. "And you should probably talk to Lucky."

From the look he gave her, Sofia was certain Savage knew about the mating scent. As tight-lipped as the Guardians were about business, they were bad at keeping their mouths shut about matings. It wasn't that they liked to gossip. No, it was more that they prided themselves on when they found their mates and would boast about it to the others.

"About our mating scents?" she questioned, and immediately knew she'd let it slip and that wasn't what her brother was talking about when he started to growl.

"I was talking about thanking him for sweeping off your porch, but now I guess I should be asking him what his intentions are with you."

"Oh, calm down, Savage," she dismissed. Waving her hand and turning for the kitchen to grab another cup of coffee, she shook her head and explained, "We didn't touch, and we are not going to. Lucky won't come close to me, because he thinks I have feelings for Malaki."

"Well, do you?" her brother pressed.

"Not like everyone thinks," she sighed. "He's my *friend*, and we don't have any romantic notions toward each other. We just genuinely get along. Is that so hard for people to understand?"

"He hasn't been the best brother to his sister," Savage pointed out.

"I know that," Sofia sniffled, knowing what she knew about the time they had been held captive before being rescued by the Shaw pride. "He has a lot of issues."

"He did," Savage replied.

"Did?" Sofia caught his words. "You said, "did." Has he changed?"

"Well, yeah." He nodded. "Malaki is…different now. More mature. A lot more than he was a year ago, but there's just something about him that makes me wonder if he's truly over everything."

"Well, he's been through a lot," she reminded him. "You just can't get over the things he saw and did as a teenager."

"He was very respectful when he showed up here this morning," Savage admitted with a shrug. "Maybe things will be different this time."

What happened to make him change enough that even her brother outwardly spoke something nice about the male?

Was it a female? Had he found his mate? The elders have always said that when a male finds his true mate, it centers them. Could Malaki have finally found someone who loved him?

A foreign pain built in her chest. The thought of Malaki being with a female made Sofia feel…weird.

Chapter 3

*M*alaki could see her cabin from the window in his room at the old Guardian dorm. The building still held the same feeling of home that it once had, but now, it'd been updated for guests or new pride members to have temporary living space.

There were no other shifters living in the building, so he had it all to himself. He picked the room so he could watch for Sofia. Talon had ordered him to sleep as long as he needed after the early morning arrival and shift after pledging himself to the pride again.

However, he didn't sleep more than an hour. When he woke, the sun was lighting up the eastern sky and, even though he didn't need the light, it helped him see Lucky Cooper standing on the porch of his old cabin, sweeping off the snow that had piled up overnight.

It was inevitable that she would find a mate, and from the looks of it, Lucky must be the male that fate picked for her.

The old Malaki would've confronted him and told him to get off his porch if he'd never left, but being in the swamps of Louisiana changed him...a lot.

Well, not a lot. He still had issues he needed to work through regarding the things he'd seen as a teenage boy. His sister, Calla, had found herself the perfect mate. And during his time away, he'd prayed to the gods every night that Taze would heal her.

When he arrived early that morning, every single Guardian was there to welcome him home as if he'd been a gold star member when he'd lived there before.

The first male to seek him out was Taze, and it surprised him that the male, who was once his enemy, gave him a welcoming pat on the back and a respectful handshake. It was shocking, but by the time he was passed around to everyone, he realized he was home again.

Granted, he'd been in talks with Talon since he'd shown up unannounced two months ago. There were a lot of rules set in place concerning him and his desire to return. Talon wanted him to take a little more time to work on himself before rejoining the pride, and that was what he did.

The Khat drug trade in Louisiana had been taken care of after the last wolf alpha had been apprehended.

Lucky

He stayed at the pride he worked for and did jobs around their lands to keep his body busy while his mind healed. If it wasn't for the newly turned wolf, Nixon, and his background, Malaki wouldn't be back. He would've stayed the same as he'd always been.

He would never forget the things he saw regarding his sister, but he'd learned to move past it, just as she'd done on her own. He held a lot of guilt for the way he had treated her, too. The only way he could resolve that issue was to see her, and that was his plan for the morning. After he saw Calla, he'd head over to visit with Sofia.

He showered and combed out his long, dirty blond hair, remembering when he'd kept it short and cut tight to his head. After being drug around by his hair as a teen, he'd cut it all off because of the memories. Growing it out was another way of healing.

He slipped on his boots and made his way down the stairs and out the door. Trudging through the snow, he headed toward his sister's cabin up the gravel road. Thankfully, no one was outside to see him. He didn't want people to stare even though they had every right to wonder why he was there again.

The Guardians were friendly when he'd returned, but the other pride members would be shocked, and honestly, a little worried to see him back. It would take time for them to accept him, and he knew it, but his new outlook on life made him okay with their worry. If he was in their shoes, he'd be worried, too. He was by no means a different male. He still had his demons to work through.

Two seconds after he knocked on the door to his sister's cabin, her mate, Taze, opened the door. He smiled widely and nodded for Malaki to come in. The moment Calla peeked her head around the corner, she gasped, "*Malaki!*"

His baby sister…the one he protected as best as he could when they were too young to know the dangers of the world, ran into his arms and cried his name over and over.

"Shhh, now. It's okay," Malaki cooed as he held her tight, relaxing as his body and panther knew he'd made the right decision to finally come home. "I love you, sister mine, and I'm sorry for the way I treated you. It's time for us to be a family again."

Even with the words falling from his lips, he wondered if he'd ever be a normal male and have his own family like everyone else. Regardless of his issues, he loved his sister more than himself, and he wanted to try to make things right again with her and her new mate.

Sofia was going out of her mind. It was noon and she still hadn't seen Malaki. She hadn't seen Lucky, either.

She knew Lucky was working with the other Guardians to clear the lands and get wood to every single cabin for the pride to have warmth.

Liberty had started a group chat on her cell phone

Lucky

with the members of the pride several months ago, and she offered the main house and the dorms for anyone who needed to leave their homes for the night. Weather reports were getting worse by the hour and by midnight, the area was expecting negative temperatures.

For northern Mississippi, that was unheard of, but the pride had a plan, and she'd responded to the alpha's mate to let her know she would be okay overnight. Sofia knew if it got too cold, she could shift or make the trek through the snow to get to the main house at any time during the night. The doors were always open. When you were a shifter, there was no need for locked doors, and since the land was protected by the pride, no one would be walking up to the door unannounced. Plus, Talon had cameras installed all over the place.

Since she'd woken up, the snow totals had gone from four inches to ten, and while the cubs and teenagers loved it, she wasn't quite ready to join them. It was beautiful until someone made tracks through it, though. In their area, snow only lasted a day, but this winter storm wasn't going to melt by morning. No, it was going to be a week-long event.

After her coffee, she paced the living room floor, almost wearing a hole in the maroon rug beneath her feet. Her human mind was on Malaki while her panther one was on Lucky. She wanted to call both of them, but decided it would be best if she just stayed put.

The knock on the door startled her, and she jumped when she heard his voice on the other side, "Sofia, it's me…Mal."

She ran to the door as tears built in her eyes. The moment she opened the door, she gasped at the change in the male she'd considered one of her closest friends. Since he'd left a year ago, his hair had grown. It was past his shoulders, and the childish bright blonde had dulled to a darker, dirtier color. He still looked like the Malaki she'd grown up with, but the war with the rogues had changed him, and she could see it in his eyes. It didn't matter to her, though. He was home.

At that point, she didn't care anymore about the no touching rule the Guardians and males of the pride lived by. Plus, she already knew who her destined mate was, and they hadn't made any contact. So, she was free to touch any male she chose. With that in mind, Sofia jumped at him, engulfing him in a tight hold as his long hair tickled her arms. "Oh, my gods, you're home!"

"Woah," he warned, stiffening beneath her. "Why did you touch me?" The male who'd been her best friend for so long took her by the shoulders and pushed her away.

"Who fucking cares at this point?" Okay, she was mad now. "Why haven't you come home? Why haven't you answered my calls?"

"It's complicated," he hedged, pointing toward the cabin. "Let's go inside. It's cold as fuck out here."

He'd changed so much since the last time she'd seen him. His face had matured. Whatever he'd been doing down south had changed him, and she had a feeling it was in more ways than just age.

"Do you want some coffee?" She had no idea what to offer him, and she placed a palm to her forehead. "Hell, this is your cabin. You should be welcome to anything."

"Sofia, it's not my cabin," he sighed, looking around. "I gave this to you for a reason."

"You did?" she asked, confused.

"It was time for you to learn to live on your own," he said softly. "A female needs her independence, and I thought you'd like to have the peace and quiet of being in the new housing area since my...your cabin was the first one."

Sofia did love the peace and quiet of the cabin. The only noise she heard was from anyone going to the old dorms to use the gym for training, but that wasn't very often since she worked full time at the animal clinic.

"We should talk," he said, waving off the offer of something to drink. Instead, he took a seat in the recliner she used, but she didn't care. Sitting at the end of the couch, she folded her legs under her and waited for him to say something, but he just...didn't.

"Mal, you're my friend," she reminded him. "Whatever you need to say, say it."

His eyes sparked amber as he looked at her with a heat she'd only seen from one other male, and her heart thundered in her chest. Malaki was nothing like he'd been when he came to the pride a broken young male. Now, he was built like a fucking tank, and his long, dirty blond hair covered half of his face. He looked more like a Guardian than he ever did when he was living at the Shaw pride.

"Look, I wanted to clear the air with you," he began, rubbing his temple. "We were friends, and things have changed...*I've* changed."

"I can see that," she responded, swallowing down the question she had about him saying they were friends...in the past tense.

"As you well know, word spreads quickly around here, and I already know about the mating scent the last time I was here. I need to make it clear to you that the scent in the air was not mine."

"Oh, Malaki," she breathed. "I know. It took a long time, but I just recently realized it wasn't yours. It'd been driving me insane for the last two months, trying to figure it out. That all changed yesterday when Lucky came over to deliver firewood."

"I just want you to be happy, and I want you to be protected by him," he warned, narrowing his eyes. "We all know I wasn't the favorite Guardian here for a long time. I was a complete asshole, but I've been working through my trauma."

"That's a good thing," she reminded him. "I'm proud of you, Mal."

"I talked to my sister today, and we are good." He cracked a rare smile. "We are going to spend more time together and become a family again."

"So, you're staying? For good?" she cheered.

Lucky

"I am," he said as he nodded. "I just wanted you to know that even though we are not ever going to be mates, I love you as a friend, and I want you to not worry about me. I'm going to be okay."

"Are you sure?" she pressed, knowing him better than anyone besides his sister. "You have a lot of resentment."

"I did...still do," he admitted. "I met a male in New Orleans, and we actually became friends. He was a therapist before the wolves turned him. He decided to stay there and learn his new life, living with the pride. This male, a wolf of all things, helped me through a lot of the shit that made me the jerk I was since I became of age."

"I'm so glad," she sniffled as her shoulders dropped. "The Shaw pride has always loved you, and I know everyone tried to give you and Calla a normal life after you two were rescued. It just wasn't the right time for you to live here. I believe in fate, and I honestly think you leaving for Louisiana was probably the right thing for you."

"That's why we are friends, Sofia," he chuckled. "You always were smarter than me."

"Oh, shut up, Mal," she giggled, feeling all of the weight of his anger lift from her own shoulders. She'd worn his angst as her own for so long, because they had such a tight bond.

But it wasn't the mating bond...even though she did love him.

However, there was still something there, deep in his icy blue stare that worried her. It didn't matter that he said he was better, she could see it. He was trying to return to the only home he knew, making amends with his sister, but Sofia sensed he would carry those memories for the rest of his life. What he'd seen just didn't go away with therapy.

Chapter 4

"*You need to sit your* ass right fucking there, Lucky," Storm warned.

Lucky's panther was on the prowl, and his brother was keeping him from going over to Sofia's and beating the shit out of Malaki for even stepping foot in her cabin. He had no idea what the male was doing inside her cabin…well, Malaki's cabin.

The human side of him knew the two of them were friends, but his mating scent and his panther didn't want the male around his mate. He didn't care if Malaki had returned a changed male. He didn't trust him.

"I don't want him touching her," he growled.

"Yeah, you don't even have to tell me that." Storm rolled his eyes. "I can scent you from a mile away," Lucky grunted and rolled his eyes at his brother.

"How did you deal with this shit before you touched Amaya?" Lucky was going to go insane now that Sofia knew he was the one giving off the mating scent that day at the alpha's home. If he were a lesser male, and had no chivalry, he would've just touched her the moment he knew, but he didn't.

"Well, I didn't do well," Storm chuckled as his cub, Dash, started to cry from the other room. Amaya emerged with the cub in hand, stopping at the threshold of the living room. "Everything okay?"

It was time for his nephew to be fed, and that was Lucky's clue to get out. He didn't want to waste his brother's time with his mate. "I'm going to head out. We can talk later."

"Be careful," Storm hollered as Lucky reached the door. "They're calling for a few more inches this afternoon."

"I'm going to plow the driveway and roads to the cabins again later today," he offered and stepped out into the freezing morning air. His breath puffed out in little clouds as his eyes narrowed on the cabin across the alpha's backyard. Malaki was leaving, and he and Sofia were both smiling widely.

As much as the male had matured, Lucky still didn't like him because he was too close to Sofia. Sofia wasn't like most of the other females…the ones who'd become Protectors of the pride. She had no desire to learn to fight, and that was okay with him. He wanted to be the one to care for and protect her…not let some wayward

Lucky

Guardian with an attitude keep her from harm.

It didn't take long for Malaki to see Lucky trekking through the snow, heading for her cabin. Lucky smirked a little at knowing he'd been the one to clear off her porch right as the first rays of light turned the pride's land from darkness that morning.

"Lucky," Malaki greeted, holding out his hand for a shake. On instinct, Lucky extended his hand and nodded.

"Malaki," he replied, gritting his teeth against the cold and the desire to just punch him. "Welcome back."

"Before you try and beat my ass, I just want you to know that Sofia and I have talked." Malaki manned up. "She is one of the only people who believed in me growing up here, and she is my friend, but nothing else. I know you are her mate, and I give you my honor that I have no intentions of changing her mind about you."

"Huh, really?" Lucky huffed. "I didn't know she was making a choice."

"She isn't, because we are just friends," Malaki repeated as he pulled a knit cap over his head, letting his long hair curl around the base of his neck. "I said what I needed to say to her, and I'm sure she could use a visit from you."

"Honestly, Malaki," Lucky said with narrowed eyes, "I haven't even begun to trust you. The last time I saw you, you were just the same asshole you were when you originally left. So, pardon me if I don't give a fuck what you tell me about the female who is going to be my mate someday."

"I get it," Malaki agreed, and that just pissed Lucky off. He really wanted to punch the fucker for all the years he'd caused so much pain to the pride. "I won't be a problem to you anymore."

And with that, the male walked off as if they'd just had a normal conversation.

"What the fuck?" Lucky whispered. He knew the male had changed, but he also knew that no one could get over the things he'd seen and been through over the course of a few months. What changed him from two months ago when he'd returned to speak with Talon? Something didn't add up.

He watched Malaki walk off for only a few seconds before he turned toward the single cabin on the new road on the other side of the property. The snow was piling up again when he climbed the three steps to Sofia's porch. He would care for her place later, and from the looks of the radar, he'd need to do all of the properties again before nightfall.

He didn't even knock before Sofia pulled the door open. She had tears in her eyes, and he wanted to take her into his arms, but what came out of his mouth was more anger than worry.

"What did he say to you?" Gods, he could scent the male on her, and his eyes flashed amber. Malaki's scent was everywhere.

"Nothing," she promised, placing her hand over her heart. "I'm just a little emotional. I wasn't expecting him to be so…okay…but *not*. Come in, Lucky. It's freezing outside."

"Let me fill up your wood supply first," he offered, needing something to do with his hands. If he didn't, he'd go find Malaki and choke him for making her cry, and from the scent burning his nose, he knew they'd touched.

As he sat the wood in the holder by her stove, she took a seat in the recliner that scented of the other male. Lucky had to tamp down his panther and remember the female wasn't quite his…yet.

"Want to talk about it?" he asked, knowing damn well he was being nosy.

"There's not much to talk about." She shrugged and pulled a crocheted blanket over her lap. "He came by to talk, and we worked things out when he admitted he knew you were my mate."

"Worked things out?" Lucky snarled. "I can scent him on you, Sofia. Did he touch you?"

"No," she growled. "I touched him. I knew it wouldn't do anything if I did, and I was so damn happy to see him. I hugged him, and then we talked."

"About?" He was not fucking happy about their touching.

"It's not my story to tell, but he's changed, and I hope everyone understands that," she announced. "Let him get adjusted to being back, and I'm sure you'll see it, too."

"So, he is staying?" Lucky asked, growling again when she nodded. Well, he didn't growl. The sound coming from him was strictly his panther. It was agitated.

"He's my friend, Lucky," she reminded him. "You're going to have to get over it and understand that we had a bond before he even left. We worked together for a long time, and he connected with me more than anyone else in this pride. He's a good male, but he just had a lot of baggage when he arrived. You, and everyone else, need to put yourself in his shoes and think about how you would react to the hell he and Calla had been through…the things he'd seen at such a young age."

Lucky did know about the things Malaki had seen while trying to protect his sister when he was only a young teenager. Calla was younger than him, and she'd had some terrible trauma, but she got past that when she mated Taze. Malaki almost ruined that for his sister, too.

"You're right," he agreed, but only to the truths she mentioned. "Malaki didn't grow up here, and he was new to us for a long time. His attitude didn't help when we were training him, either. Gods, he was such a jerk."

"Yes, he was." She shook her head like she was trying to dislodge her thoughts. "Can I make you something to eat?"

"No, thank you," he replied and walked over to add a log to her dying fire. "It's cold in here, Sofia. You need to keep the place warm so your pipes don't freeze."

"I like the cold weather, and I forgot about the plumbing." She blushed and crinkled her nose. "It's easier to shift when I'm cold, and I've never owned my own place before."

"Do you want to take a run with me?" he asked, looking at his watch. "I'm off work today and have a lot of free time before the next round of snow hits." With his words, he scented himself, and knew she could recognize his mating scent as it filled the air. The moment her own made its appearance, they'd both moved a bit closer, but Lucky stepped back when he realized they were too close.

"We need to talk about this," he blurted.

"We do," she agreed. "Maybe we could run later?"

"I'd like that, a lot," he agreed.

Sofia pulled her long, brown hair up into a messy bun and poured herself another cup of coffee after Lucky denied her after she offered him a cup. She wanted to care for him, but he wouldn't accept anything, and it was making her panther prowl. All it wanted was for her to touch the male and make their mating official.

She'd known him her entire life, and she knew they would be mates now that the truth was out. The problem was, what would happen after they touched? She knew he had his own place, and she'd end up living with him, but a little part of her didn't want to give up Malaki's cabin unless he wanted it back.

Which was the dumbest reason for not wanting to touch her mate.

"Look." She took a seat at the small table by the kitchen. "We don't need to dance around the subject. We are mates. It's obvious by our scents."

Lucky held up his hand to stop her. "Like I told you before, I'm not going to compete with Malaki for you."

"Malaki is not your competition," she growled. With a firm conviction, she slammed her fist on the tabletop to get her point across. "We are nothing but friends. He and I have a bond, but it's not like what you think."

"Then explain it to me, princess." He swallowed hard. She liked it when he called her by the nickname. It made her body warm to him even more. "Because I just don't understand why he only treated you with respect. He didn't even treat his own alpha with respect when he was here. And now, I can scent him all over you. It's driving me insane."

"I love him, but not like you think," she admitted, holding up her hand when his eyes flashed amber. "As a friend, Lucky. Just a friend. He was my Guardian during the issue with the wolves. We talked more than he ever talked with anyone else in this pride. He took his role as Guardian seriously during that time, and he worried for me when we were at the office. He wouldn't let me go anywhere without checking the room first. He hated the rogues just as much as everyone else. He left us to go help other prides fight them, and when he left, he cut us all off. It hurt me…bad."

"Do you want to be his mate?" he choked out.

Lucky

"Never," she promised. "I never felt anything more than friendly love toward him. At one point, he was my best friend. That's it. Right now, I'm more concerned about you and our connection."

"And how do you feel about our mating scents?" he pressed. She wasn't mad at him for his questions, and she knew he was feeling out her concern over Malaki.

"I actually dream about you," she whispered. "I want to find my mate and be the best female to my fated mate, and that mate is you, Lucky."

"I'm not going to force the touch, Sofia," he admitted, holding up his hand to stop her from talking. "Once you decide, it will be you who initiates the touch and the mating. I won't do that to you."

"You are a very respectful male, Lucky," she said with a smile, but it was fake. She wanted him to do it…to touch her. She wanted to feel the frenzy of a first mating, the bite and the blood of her mate, and she wanted to experience his strength. "I need some time, though. I don't know if I'm ready. I'd like to spend more time with you, though."

"I'd like that, too," he agreed. "So, how about that run?"

"How deep is the snow?"

"About eight inches," he beamed. "They're expecting at least another two inches over the next few hours."

"My cat really likes the snow whenever we do get a lot here," she revealed. Northern Mississippi only got snow this deep once every five or more years. She barely remembered the last time she'd seen that much snow on the ground, and then, she was only a cub.

"So does mine."

"Let's go run," she cheered.

"You shift, and I'll meet you on the porch," he laughed. The excitement was infectious.

Lucky stepped out on the porch to shift, leaving her cabin door cracked just slightly so she could paw at the door in her panther form. When she was ready, he waited in the snow at the bottom of the steps. Her panther raised up and used her mouth to softly bite the door handle to shut the cabin door.

Lucky's panther huffed to get her attention and walked around the back of her cabin. There was a trail there that was hardly used, but it was wide enough they could run through it without any issues. In the woods, the snow wasn't as deep, but that didn't mean that it wasn't impassable. The cubs and teenage panthers had already made trails where trails weren't even cut through the land. It was exciting and cold, but the panthers didn't care.

She may not have cared for the tracks the cubs and other panthers had made through the snow that morning, but by the time they had run the trails, her panther was loving every moment of it. Thankfully, she didn't feel the cold. The warmth from the animal's coat kept her from worrying over the temperatures, which were well below freezing.

Lucky

A few teenagers had run past them, leaving the trails to roll and play down in the small valleys to her left. They were coming of age, and they liked to play fight. It was normal for them, because their nature was preparing them for the possibility of being Guardians one day.

Lucky was always there, using his animal body as a shield if they got close, and it was endearing. She liked the way he would protect her without making a scene. He never snarled at them or even bared his fangs. No, he was just respectful, and it made her mating scent thicken.

There were a few times when his panther would watch her with heat in its eyes. She knew what the animal and human side of the male was thinking, and she'd be lying if she denied having the same ideas in her mind. The panther that ruled her wanted him to touch her…just finish the mating and let the relationship come later.

It was a strange life, and nothing like human dating. She'd heard that humans usually dated for a year or longer before even deciding if the person they were seeing was the one they wanted to spend eternity with, but for shifters, it was different. If she was smart, she would take Lucky back to her cabin and initiate the touch to just get things started, but he was right. She had a lot of things she needed to get straight in her life concerning Malaki before she could devote her attention to the male who was chosen for her.

Lucky was going to be her mate, and her panther knew it. Hell, *she* knew it.

Theresa Hissong

But why was she hesitant?

Was it her brother's grumpiness over any male touching his baby sister? Or was it the idea that once she touched Lucky, she'd never be able to make contact with Malaki?

Maybe it was because she was simply scared and unaware of how to even be with a male.

There was so much she needed to work through before she made the decision to touch him.

Malaki, being one of them. Her feelings for him were simply friendly, but there was more, and she didn't understand it. Lucky was her true mate, but they weren't really close before he'd released his mating scent. Why was the mating scent just now showing up? Why did their nature take so long?

When they returned to her cabin, they shifted separately, and she respected him for letting her have her time alone to dress. Even though nudity was a normal thing, it changed when there was a possible mating involved. The males were respectful and let the females dress alone.

"Would you like to come to my place to have some lunch?" he asked.

She shivered from the thought of being alone with him in his cabin, and he mistook it for the cold. "I have soup. You're freezing. Come on, princess."

He turned to walk away, and she found herself following him through the small trail someone had dug out across the back of the alpha's home. Her eyes widened in surprise when she realized he'd done it. "Did you come over and clean off my porch early this morning?"

"Actually, yes." He paused while she stopped to look around. "I plowed the roads to the cabins, too."

"That was very thoughtful of you, Lucky," she blushed. "Thank you."

"I didn't want you to slip and fall," he reminded her. "Come, let's eat. It's starting to snow again."

White flakes were falling from the cloudy skies once more, and the sound of it hitting the limbs on the trees was one of the most peaceful sounds she'd ever heard. Like a soft rain, but not quite, each flake sounded like specks of glass sprinkling against the already covered ground. "I love the sound the snow makes."

"Hm," he grunted. "I've never noticed it."

"Sometimes, you have to listen to what Mother Nature gives us," Sofia mentioned. "The earth is in our blood, and...I don't know. I just respect it. Forgive me...I'm rambling." Gods, she sounded stupid. She loved being outside, and she loved the woods, the water, and even the snow.

"You can tell me anything, Sofia," he offered, his brows pinching forward in thought. "I don't think you're rambling, by the way. You love what you love, and I enjoy listening to you tell me those things."

"Thanks, Lucky," she beamed.

He was a good male. When he was younger, much younger, he was quite the handful. Or, at least, that was what she'd heard her brother saying to Mary Grace one night while she was over at their cabin to visit with their cubs.

A little part of her didn't want him to be so sweet. You could see how powerful he was just by his size. Just like all Guardians, he was a force of strength and training, and it showed as he walked ahead of her to climb the steps to his porch. His thighs were thick and they bunched and stretched as he moved. His shoulders were wide, and she'd seen how sculptured his arms and abs were last summer when he was out working on the property.

"Sofia?" he interrupted her thoughts.

"Oh, um…what? Did you say something?" She hid the blush on her face as she took off her coat and hung it by the door.

"I didn't say anything, but I can scent you." He came closer, but he didn't make a move to touch her.

"You're mating scent is mixing in the air with your arousal."

Chapter 5

Lucky wanted to touch her. He yearned to throw out his personal rules and take the female into his arms. He'd dreamed of her full lips on his for so long, he swore he already knew how they tasted.

But a blast of worry from his alpha made both of them stumble.

"Oh, gods," Sofia gasped, clutching her chest.

"Fuck, Talon!" Lucky barked as he regained his footing. "Something's wrong, Sofia. Stay here, and don't you dare leave this cabin until you hear from me or one of the Protectors."

He didn't have time to wait for her reply, praying she listened to him. Something was wrong, and from the push of power Talon just sent out, it was bad.

Every Guardian, even Malaki, burst through the back door of the alpha's home and marched into his office, wondering what had caused the ripple through the pride.

"Shut the door," Talon ordered. Kraven shut the door, throwing the lock. All of the Guardians and Protectors were there, each of them in different forms of their partial shift. Lucky's eyes were glowing amber, and his canines were sharp in his mouth. His only thought was Sofia, and if what Talon had to say meant a threat to her.

"What's going on?" Winter, his alpha's right-hand man, barked.

"There's a small panther community just west of Nashville that has been attacked by wolves," Talon cursed. "They fucking killed almost all of their Guardians and the alpha. I need a team to go in and rescue who's left and bring them here."

A round of curses lit up the room as several of the Guardians stepped forward. Jade and Evie also made themselves available.

"I need at least two Protectors to help the females. Some of them have lost their mates and cannot be touched by the Guardians just yet. They are hurt, and their healer was one of the ones killed. Landon will go with you to provide medical attention. You need to leave in the next hour…if not sooner." After your mate died, it could take months before the remaining one could handle touch from a male. It was a tricky subject, and even though the mating bond would eventually fade, the pride was too respectful to test the theory. No one wanted a widowed female in pain.

There was a ton of commotion as the Guardians and Protectors made their plans. Storm stopped Lucky on his way out the door. "It's probably best if you stay close to your mate. I'm going with the team, and we will need the dorms prepared for their arrival."

Lucky gave Storm a knowing nod. It was probably best he shouldn't leave on this assignment given the fact that he hadn't mated with Sofia yet and Malaki was in the dorms. His panther wouldn't like the separation.

"That means you're going to have to work with Malaki on this," Storm announced with a lowered voice.

"Lucky?" Talon called out as everyone was filing out of his office. Storm jutted his chin out toward the alpha, knowing what Talon would say to him.

"Sir?"

"I heard what Storm said, and I agree," he began, waiting for the last of the Guardians to exit the room. Storm waited until they were gone to be the last one out the door, closing it as he went.

"You want me to stay on the property?" he confirmed.

"Son, you need to understand that a male who is in the possible early stages of a mating can't be separated from their mate," Talon advised. "It's in your best interest, and hers, if you stay close to the pride. I know you'd love to go help, but I just can't authorize that right now."

Talon was more than just an alpha...he was wise beyond his years. Lucky nodded in agreement and held out his hand, "Thank you, alpha."

"Take care of the dorms, and I assure you Malaki will do everything he can to help," Talon ordered. "You two work together to get five rooms ready, and I will have the females start making food to fill the kitchen there."

"Will do," he agreed, praying the new arrivals were okay.

"Remember, this is important," Talon reminded him right before he turned to leave the office, and Lucky felt the push of his powers, making what he said a soft order.

"Yes, sir."

He left the alpha's home in a hurry, running toward Sofia's cabin after he'd realized she'd disobeyed him and headed to her own home. His boots slipped on the new snow that had gathered on the steps, but he didn't miss a beat as he climbed the porch. When he already scented Malaki in the house, his panther was on edge, and that just set him off.

Pushing the door open without caring to knock, he was slightly relieved that Malaki was across the room from Sofia, but the tears in her eyes sent him into a near frenzy.

"What are you doing here?" he demanded, moving around the male to stand in front of his potential mate. His eyes fell on hers. "Why did you leave my cabin?"

Lucky

There was a yearning to grab Sofia and pull her almost under his skin. Malaki's eyes were glowing amber, and rightly so. News had been released of the pride who'd been slaughtered by wolves. The same wolves the Shaw pride had thought were eradicated.

"Sofia?" Lucky growled.

"I'm fine. I thought I'd be safer at my home until I heard what the alpha had called you for," she sniffled and held up her hand. "Malaki explained, and he said he didn't know how long you were going to be held up in the alpha's office and came over to ask me to help with getting the new members set up in the old dorms."

"Why are you crying?" he barked, narrowing his eyes on Malaki. Gods, his panther was wanting a fight with the returned Guardian, and that had to stop. Guardians getting into fights over a female was frowned upon. More than frowned upon, actually. It was damn near forbidden.

"Because this is awful," she replied, wiping her eyes. Her long, brown hair was pulled up into a messy bun, and she tightened the band around it. "We just found peace again, and now we know there are more out there."

"The wolves won't come here," Malaki promised with a raised hand. Lucky shook his head to tell the Guardian not to promise such things that were out of his control, but the fool kept talking. "The Shaw pride is too strong for something like this to happen."

"I pray to the gods that we are," she replied and

turned for the coat rack by her front door. She donned a thick jacket and grabbed her boots. "Let's go prepare. I need something to do to keep my mind off what is about to happen here."

Malaki excused himself and as he passed Lucky, his eyes were still throwing amber sparks. "I'll gather the food from the females."

Within the next hour, Malaki and the females were rushing into the kitchen of the dorms, filling the fridge full of food. When the door opened, Lucky scented the meats cooking on the massive grill out back behind the alpha's home. His stomach rumbled from the lack of food. It seemed like forever since he'd had a meal. He was supposed to provide for Sophia before the alpha called out to him, and he wondered if she'd eaten anything.

He used his senses and found her in one of the upstairs rooms bent over while she put a fitted sheet on one of the beds. His cock hardened at the sight, and he adjusted himself right before she turned around.

"Hey," she said as she finished making the bed.

"You should eat, Sofia," he announced. "The females have already brought some food for the new arrivals." He didn't mention that Malaki had been a part of that brigade of food delivery, either. Just saying the male's name aloud left a bad taste in his mouth.

Lucky

"That food is for them." She shook her head. "I can get something later. There's too much to do before then."

"Princess," he sighed. "Come. Let's eat something."

She climbed off the corner of the bed and stood, lowering her eyes. "Why do you call me princess?"

"Because that's what you are to me," he admitted, scenting her arousal. "Do you not like that?"

"Actually, I do," she blushed and moved toward him. "Gods, Lucky, I want to touch you, but now just isn't the right time."

"We have all the time in the world," he promised. "I'm not going anywhere."

With a nod, she reached for a comforter and tossed it on the bed with expert precision, watching as it softly covered the bed. A few more arrangements and she was done. "I have three more rooms to do."

"Need some help?" he asked.

"Actually, I'd prefer you help me make sure there are enough supplies in the bathrooms," she grinned. "And make sure the toilets are clean."

He grumbled, but did as he was asked, keeping his senses on alert for the female wherever she was in the upstairs part of the dorms. If she even dared to head downstairs, he would know it, and he would follow to make sure Malaki wasn't there, either.

Her care for the new panthers that were coming was endearing. She'd always been one of the first females to volunteer whenever it came to helping the pride or preparing meals for a solstice or equinox gathering. He loved that about her.

Most of the females in the pride were starting to learn to fight, but Sofia enjoyed her life as it was, and a large part of Lucky liked the fact she was so feminine. Not that it was a bad thing. Sofia was a strong female in so many ways, but she enjoyed her time helping instead of fighting. It made him want to protect her more, and his panther rumbled in agreement.

He should touch her…he really should. It was almost time to make the mating complete. It was obvious they were both on board, but there was one thing…one male in the way.

Malaki.

While he worked, females would come up the stairs to check and see if they needed any help. At one point, Marie, Evie's mother, tried to shoo him out of the dorms, but he wouldn't budge. "I'm fine, Ms. Marie. I'd like to stay where I am."

The elder female didn't miss his glance toward the room where Sofia was working on another bed.

"I understand." She winked and left them alone.

For the next two hours, so many people were coming and going that he lost track of Sofia after he'd gone outside to cut up more wood for the dorm's fireplace. Sofia had done everything she could to make sure the guests would be comfortable until Talon could figure out where to put them or offer them a spot in the pride, and he was impressed by her willingness to do things for shifters she didn't even know.

Lucky

"There you are," she huffed, dropping a basket of books and magazines on the coffee table in the main living area.

"Where have you been?" he asked, but a growl behind him stopped him from continuing.

"Mal," Sofia held up her hand in warning, "don't."

"Don't what?" Lucky barked, looking between the two of them. "What's his problem?"

"You should talk to her like a worthy female…which she is," Malaki accused, narrowing his eyes. "Instead of throwing harsh questions at her. She's been working hard just like the rest of us."

Lucky stepped up without thought, getting right in his face. "Look, don't you dare come back here and act like you have any claim to her. If you'd let me finish my sentence, you would've known that I wasn't being harsh. I'd advise you to back the fuck off before we start having problems, again."

"Please…please don't do this," Sofia begged, tears choking her voice. She ran up to the two males, trying to get between them without touching either one. And as soon as she got close, they separated.

"Come on, princess," Lucky smirked in Malaki's direction. "I was looking for you so I could make sure you had some food before everyone arrives. They'll be here soon."

"Good idea," she blurted, turning toward Malaki. "Go on and wait for them to arrive. Let us know when they are ten minutes away."

Malaki turned on his heel like a scolded dog. It satisfied Lucky that he'd used the endearment in public for the first time. It wasn't only Malaki who'd heard it, either. All of the females were in the kitchen frozen with joy on their faces. As soon as he held his hand out for Sofia to go ahead of him, the elder females started working around the area, making them both a plate.

"I need to wash up," he announced, waiting for June and Marie to step out of the way so he could use the sink. "Go ahead and eat, Sofia."

She picked up a fork and glanced down at her plate, but not before he caught a sexy smile playing at the corner of her lip.

Chapter 6

*S*ofia *tried to hide her* arousal at the way Lucky talked and cared for her, and she wanted to melt every single time he called her princess. The blush she felt on her cheeks was more from the other women seeing them interact. It was her first time being with any male, and finding out they were reacting to each other's mating scents made her heart flutter. She liked it.

However, Malaki did not, and to be honest, Lucky was right. Mal had no claim to her, because they were not mates, and they would never be anything more than friends. His outburst earlier appalled her. He should've never done that, and he was spared the wrath of Lucky. She really thought the two were going to physically fight, and she wouldn't be able to stop them. It was time she finalized her feelings for Malaki, and sat him down to explain how thankful she was for his friendship, but if he was going to act jealous when Lucky was around, their friendship would suffer.

And she didn't want that.

There would be a time and place for a talk with Malaki, but it wouldn't be that night. The temperatures were dropping, and there was still a lot of snow on the ground, but from all the running around, she was almost overheated. The trip to the other pride should only take three hours, but it would be a slow return for the Guardians and Protectors as they made their way back to the pride house. As it was, the sun was setting already, and everyone was in for a long, cold night.

Lucky took the seat at the head of the table and paused before he began to eat. The males liked to make sure their mates were fed before they nourished themselves, and Sofia rolled her eyes. She finished a bite of food and pointed her fork toward his plate. "You need to eat too. Don't wait on me to finish."

He grunted in frustration but took a bite of his food, and she tried to ignore the way a lock of his dark blond hair fell across his forehead. She was almost full anyway, and she wanted to go over the dorm one more time before everyone arrived to make sure she hadn't forgotten anything. Having something to do would keep her mind off of him…maybe.

"I'm going to double-check all of the rooms while you finish eating," she said as she stood with her plate. Marie took it from her to wash, and she could feel his icy

Lucky

blue eyes on her as she left the room.

Each step up to the second floor felt like she was being torn away from Lucky. The feelings her panther had been feeding her over the last twenty-four hours told her it was getting close to the time for them to touch.

Her lower belly ached, and she shook off the desire to touch him. It was time to focus on the Guardians' return with the broken pride. Despite the rapid heartbeat in her chest and the fire between her virgin legs, she had to do the job she'd taken on for the pride.

Each room was set, extra towels were placed on the ends of the dressers, and Lucky had done a wonderful job making sure the bathrooms were clean and stocked. Now, all they had to do was wait, but voices downstairs announced the news.

By the time she reached the kitchen, Malaki, Lucky, Maire, and June were setting up the tables for food. "They'll be here in five minutes."

There wasn't much time to be prepared before trucks and a single white van arrived. Booth, Jade, and Kraven jumped out of the driver's seat of each vehicle with Axel, Landon, Hope, and Diesel by their sides. The doors opened and Sofia gasped at the five shifters who exited. Two were elder males, and three were females.

One of them looked to be close to her age, and she was scared, crying as she was held by two older females. Sofia rushed out to the van and immediately introduced herself.

"My name is Sofia Corvera, and I am here for

anything you need," she promised. "Who here is already mated?"

"We are," the elder females said in unison.

The eldest one, a short but robust female, held out her hand. Sofia took it and pressed their combined hands to her heart. "Our mates were killed, and we are so thankful for your pride coming to help us. This is Cheyenne. My name is Gianna Love, and this is my younger sister, Ella Love. We never married our mates as to human customs and kept our birth names."

"Come inside." Sofia ushered them toward the door. "We have food and beds for everyone. I'm sure our healer has checked you over, right?"

"Yes, we've mostly healed from our injuries, but Cheyenne is needing some extra help," Ella whispered, looking over her shoulder at the young female. She was in distress, but Sofia didn't have to wait long until Landon was at her side, wearing special gloves to take her over to the clinic.

"We will be back shortly," he advised, and walked Cheyenne across the alpha's backyard to Harold's clinic. Sofia didn't know exactly what had transpired at their pride, but she prayed it wasn't what she thought for the young female. Her clothes were covered in blood, but Sofia couldn't find an exact source from where it came.

"Please, let me introduce you to our other pride members." Sofia tried to remember her manners, but the ache in her lower belly wouldn't subside. She was not feeling well, but she had to be strong for the new arrivals.

Once inside, she spotted Lucky talking to the males who'd arrived. His chin jutted up into the air, and she saw him take a deep breath. He could probably scent her, and she blushed at the thought of her arousal so thick in the air.

"Sofia," June called out. "This is Ellington and Hurley Patton. They were the Patton alpha's brothers." June's eyes were full of tears, and Sofia knew what her elder female was saying. These males were not alpha material since their brother had been killed. They couldn't take over the pride, and they were in need of the Shaw pride's help.

Like a wind blasting through the trees from a hurricane, Talon Shaw entered the old dorms, his amber eyes focused on the new arrivals. He walked over, introducing himself to each and every one of them, whispering silent words of sorrow for their fallen alpha.

He looked over his shoulder, his eyes falling on hers. His head ticked to the side, but he shook whatever he was thinking away to address Sofia. "Are their rooms ready?"

"They are, sir," she replied. "Everyone has their pick."

"Let's go upstairs to get you all settled," he offered the elders.

Talon was a force any day of the week, but when it came to bringing someone new into the pride, he was even more protective, and the pride felt it down to their bones.

Something else was tingling inside her mind…inside her body. It was a heat she couldn't explain…

Lucky's scent struck her hard as Malaki entered the room. There were voices, but the ache in her belly was too strong…too potent…

Something was wrong. She didn't feel *right*.

Sofia wasn't quite sure who spoke, but she heard voices. Her best friend was frozen at the entrance to the dorm, and the male she knew to be her mate was on the other side of the room. Malaki cleared his throat, and she glanced at him. Malaki's eyes flashed amber right before he left the room. She faintly heard the front door close before Maria and June surrounded her. Lucky was moving closer, but the females got to her first.

"Lucky, could you give us a minute, please?" June asked. The older woman, who cared for the children of the pride, took Sofia by the arm and pulled her around the corner. "Are you feeling okay?"

"Not really," Sofia replied. Her eyes were locked on the kitchen where she could actually hear Lucky breathing heavily. "I feel…different."

"Oh honey," Marie gasped. "Come outside. Right now!"

In a rush, the females took her out the back door, blocking the exit as they walked into the frigid night air. Breathing was getting harder, and Sofia felt the pain in her belly. She gasped, knowing what exactly was

Lucky

happening the moment she was slapped in the face by the cold wind.

"I'm about to go into heat?" she cursed. "I can't do this…not tonight. I…can't."

"You need to go see the healer, right now," June ordered. "I'll walk you over."

"No," she cried, wanting Lucky. His scent. The need for his care. The…the everything about him. He was hers and she was his. "I want…I want…"

Her voice died on her lips when the back door crashed open, pushing Marie out of the way, but he didn't hurt her, nor did he touch her.

"Princess?" he gasped.

"No, Lucky." June tried to intervene, but Sofia started crying more. The heat…the *ache*. She'd been there before, having to be sedated during her heat the last two years, because she didn't have a mate to give her his seed. It was a curse to the females of the race who weren't mated. It was five to seven days of misery.

"June, please," Sofia begged, reaching for him.

"Sofia," Marie gave one last warning. "Either I call the healer, or you go with Lucky. It's your choice."

It was her choice, and it was going to be a fast one. She wasn't stupid, and neither was Lucky. They were mates, and their scents didn't lie.

"Leave us," Lucky ordered. The two elder females knew the word of a Guardian was as close to the alpha as one could get, and they left with one last look to make sure she was okay. On her nod, they slipped through the door. Sofia clutched her forearm to her belly.

"I'm so sorry, Lucky," she cried, "I didn't know it was happening until now."

"You have a choice to make," he began, gritting his thick canines. "It is either we go ahead and touch, or you go to the healer. This is your decision."

"But…do you want me, Lucky?" she asked, doubling over. He tried to reach for her, but she held out her hand to let him know she was okay. He could tell he took it wrong. "I need to know if you're ready."

"I've always been ready to take my mate, but with your history with *him*, I don't know if you are ready," he admitted. "You need to decide."

"I don't love him, Lucky," she admitted, tears streaming down her face. "I've never loved him. My feelings for you are new, and they're scary, but my panther…she knows…she *knows* you are the one."

"Then touch *me*, princess," he begged. "Touch me, and make me your mate."

Oh, gods.

"It's…too soon?" she cried.

"You tell me, princess," he pressed, moving closer to her. Gods, his scent was driving her mad. "Is it really too soon?"

Malaki scented his best friend's heat and immediately bolted from the Guardian's old dorms. He knew if he was anywhere in the vicinity when Lucky realized Sofia was going into heat, Lucky would fight him to claim her, and the male had every right to protect his potential mate.

It was all true though. Malaki loved Sofia, but not the way a mated male should. No, Malaki was sure he was not lovable at all. Not with the things he'd seen in his youth. There was no way to find a female who would be able to love him through all of his bullshit.

It wasn't possible.

No matter how much he'd worked through the things he'd seen and been through, he knew life as a Guardian was his only option from then until the day he died. His sister's care was now in the hands of her mate, and he'd taken almost a year to accept that.

"Malaki?" someone called out, jarring him from his thoughts. Kraven was rushing to his side. "I need your help with getting these trucks parked back in front of the house." Kraven, Hope's brother, tossed him two sets of keys.

He followed the male out to the trucks and moved them back around the property to their designated places. They were emergency vehicles, and they had to be ready at a moment's notice. Having them at the old dorms could prevent a quick escape should the pride need to evacuate.

It sucked the shifters had to be so prepared, but regardless, it was a mundane task that might actually aid them in an emergency.

As he returned to the dorms to grab another vehicle, four elder panthers were emerging from the door, heading out into the woods. Talon, in his human form, was right behind them, watching as Axel and Diesel followed them out into the land behind the alpha's home.

Malaki frowned. He thought there was another one, but he didn't see the fifth person they'd brought back from middle Tennessee. He had to finish his task and get back to see if there was anything else he needed to do in the dorms since he would be the only Guardian living there with the new arrivals. He'd inquire about the other shifter later.

"Malaki?" Kraven called out. "I still need your help."

"What else?" Malaki offered, hoping his cheery disposition would keep him from getting the same looks as before when he was an angrier Guardian.

"Landon says there is a female, a young female, named Cheyenne, who will need to run soon. Talon wants us to follow her through the woods after he gives her his blood."

"I can do that," Malaki agreed, knowing it was probably for the best that he stayed far away from Lucky and Sofia.

Chapter 7

Talon held the female's hand, "Cheyenne, you need to take my blood and shift."

"Yes...sir," she cried. Talon's voice was as soft as it could be, but the remaining scars all over the young female's body drove him and his panther insane. Those wolves had shredded her to pieces. The elder females had already changed her clothes, but she kept bleeding.

"Alpha, may I speak with you?" Harold interrupted, tilting his head to the side to let Talon know the conversation should be in private. "Before, sir."

Before meant before Talon gave Cheyenne his blood. Talon left her with Luna and stepped out into the makeshift waiting room in Harold's living area. "Talk to me."

"She should've healed by now," Harold swallowed,

looking at the closed door. "The young female may have a rare bleeding disorder for shifters. The gashes on her sides will require stitching after she shifts. I don't know if she will heal completely."

"I've heard of this," Talon groaned. "It's very rare. My aunt, who was from another pride when she mated my uncle, had it."

"There's no telling what will happen when she returns, or what her panther will heal, but I will need her to come right back here after she is ready."

Talon frowned. "That poor child."

"I know," Harold agreed, placing his calm hand on Talon's shoulder. "Please, speak to her and ask her about it. Maybe she knows about her inability to heal like everyone else."

"I need to give her my blood as soon as possible, as well." Talon paused, feeling the weight of the world on his shoulders.

"I'll wait out here," Harold offered. "The Guardians are already outside. They've shifted."

When Talon returned to the room, the poor female was being assisted by Luna, Harold's mate. They both looked up at his entrance, and Luna spoke softly to Cheyenne before excusing herself.

"Cheyenne, we must speak before you pledge yourself to my pride," Talon stated. The young, red-headed female couldn't have been older than twenty-three…maybe twenty-four. "Our healer noticed you have a disorder that is very rare in the shifter world. I need to know if you were born or changed?"

"I was born," she swallowed. Her icy blue eyes flashed amber. "I know about my medical conditions, and I know that I am not a strong blooded shifter. I've had problems my entire life, but I know my limits. I also know that I will need stitching after my shift."

"Are you able to shift?" he asked, making sure she would be healthy after he gave her his blood. The last thing he would want to do is give this female his blood and she bleeds out while her body accepted the shift. "We can stitch the wounds first."

"The stitches will dissolve when I shift after taking your blood. It's probably for the best that we wait," she replied. The poor female already knew her weaknesses, and Talon wanted nothing more than to father the young one. It made his heart ache.

"Take my blood," he began, approaching her. "There are Guardians waiting outside to follow you through your first shift. They will call out to me should you need medical aide."

"Thank you, alpha," she nodded. "I cannot thank you enough for coming to our rescue."

"I thank you for allowing the Shaw pride to come," he vowed, placing his hand over his heart and tapping it twice. "Are you ready?"

"I am," she agreed.

Talon scored his wrist and said his sacred vow, waiting until she took his blood. When it hit her system, females of the pride arrived to help her shift, and when she left the healer's clinic, the panther's fur was covered in bleeding wounds. It took everything in his power not to roar to the sky at the unfairness the female was given at birth.

Talon sent out an order to the Guardians waiting to run with the female. *She is weak. Watch her and bring her back to Harold's after her run.*

Lucky stood there watching Sofia. She was obviously in heat. The sweet scent she carried triggered every instinct he had to just mount her and give her his seed. His cock was hard as stone, and he didn't give a fuck if she, or anyone else, saw it. She needed him, and he needed her. It was time.

Well past time.

"Princess?" he whispered. "You need to make a decision, and you need to do it now. Your scent is getting stronger." His eyes were throwing amber sparks and his panther was clawing at his skin and mind. It wanted to mate…the animal wanted to take her.

A female in heat was not only cherished, but a magical thing, and as much as he wanted the frantic fucking of their connection, this was going to be different. Females went into their annual cycle to help create a new life. They weren't mated…yet, but being as their panthers already claimed each other by their scents, Lucky knew Sofia would be the one to bear his young.

Lucky

If they'd decided to touch without her being in heat, it would be different. The scenario wouldn't play out the way it was going to when he got her alone. Lucky was torn. He wanted to be gentle with her, but the heat...it drove him insane with lust just as much as he knew she was feeling it, too.

She was worried it was too soon, but Lucky already knew she was the only female he would ever want. Not because of their human connection, but because of their animal nature.

"Lucky," she breathed, still holding an arm across her lower abdomen. "I..."

"Say your words," he ordered, taking another step closer. "Tell me what you choose."

"I..."

"Say it, Sofia," he pushed. "You're in heat, and it affects me, too. When I touch you and take you as a mate, this will not be making love. We will fuck, and I will do everything in my power to make it right for you, but we are animals...you know this."

"I want that," she snarled, her eyes glowing.

"Tell me," he ordered.

"I...I choose you," she cried out as pain from her heat rolled through her body. She shivered, and sweat beaded on her brow despite the freezing temperatures outside. "Take me home, Lucky. Please..."

"Come to *me*," he pushed. "I told you that I would never force a mating, but I am begging you, princess. Touch me. Let's be done with this. We know the mating is waiting, and I promise you from tonight forward, you will be my one…my girl. I will protect and cherish you until I have no breath or blood left in my human body."

The beautiful female stumbled once, but righted herself as she closed the distance between them, reaching for his face without any hesitation. The moment their skin finally touched, bare and unhindered by any coverings, a magical connection shocked Lucky's body.

His skin was electric…like a zap of lightning had struck his soul. An invisible thread wound out of his body, mixing and tangling with her own. Her full lips took his in a frantic press, melting together when her tongue snaked out and licked over his extended canines.

"You keep doing that, and I will own your body in ways you've probably never known, princess." Lucky's voice was deep…guttural. There was a fire in his amber eyes, and he could feel his panther ordering him to mount her. Lucky pushed his panther away. Their first time should be at his cabin, and before he knew what he was doing, he had Sofia in his arms, carrying her over to his home not far from where they were standing on the alpha's back porch.

He didn't know if she'd ever been with another male, but since they'd grown up together, he knew she'd never dated anyone…not even a human male when she was in high school before the news of their existence had come out. After that, all of the kids were homeschooled. Talon didn't want anyone getting hurt or bullied in the human world. Unless she'd met a human male while working for the animal doctor, Lucky knew the night was going to be a night of firsts for his mate.

"Lucky," she panted. "I've waited for this moment for the last three years. I am untouched, but I know what I have to do to accept you."

"Do you accept me?" he pressed. So, she was untouched…a virgin. Gods, he closed his eyes and sent up a silent prayer. His mate was made for him, and he would never take that for granted.

"I accept you in all ways, Lucky," she promised, placing her hand over her heart. "Mount me…make me your mate."

His cock hardened more than he ever thought it could. "I am going to make love to you before I mount you from behind, Sofia."

She didn't wait for orders. Instead, she pulled her blue shirt from her body, revealing a white lace bra. Her breasts weren't small, nor were they big…but Lucky already knew they were the perfect size for his hands, and her nipples were dark and pebbled through the lace, yearning for his tongue.

Lucky ripped at the button on her jeans, walking her…pushing her toward his room. By the time he unzipped her pants, she was already on the covers. He didn't care about anything else in the room except for his mate.

"Lucky," she hummed as he stripped her of her jeans and panties in one swoop. He took a moment to sit back on his legs and admire her. She was curved in all the right places. Her hips were perfect for the cub they would make when he finally spilled his seed in her. This was going to be the best night he'd had in his life, and when she reached for his shirt, pulling him back to her lips, he let his animal take over.

"I want to touch you," he warned. Taking the back of his knuckle and slowly rubbing it over her pussy. He didn't breach her…no, not yet. She was wet and ready, and he gathered a small amount on his finger, bringing it to his mouth. "You taste as good as you smell, princess."

"Please, Lucky," she said as she writhed on the bed.

"Spread your legs, Sofia," he ordered. "I want to see what's mine."

She did as he'd asked and the panther inside him snarled at the sight. His jeans hit the floor alongside his shirt. His canines thickened even more in his mouth as he used his partially shifted tongue to lap at her opening.

When her hands tangled in his hair, Lucky gave up all control to his panther and feasted on her body, urging her to come on his tongue.

Sofia called his name when the release struck her body, but she wasn't done. The heat she was in demanded his seed.

"I'm going to take your virginity before I roll you over to mount you and bite you," he warned. "If I hurt you, you must tell me."

"You won't hurt me," she advised. When he held his cock in his hand, he knew that he would. She was so much smaller than him, but if the gods had given Sofia to him as a mate, he knew they would work…they'd be perfect for each other.

He positioned himself between her legs, holding his cock with one hand to guide it inside. With his other hand, he cupped her chin, forcing her eyes on his. "Look at me as I take you, princess."

She gasped at the breech, but her eyes warmed when he began to move. The moment the magic of their connection started to strengthen, Lucky leaned over and took her lips. She moaned into his mouth as her rough tongue swiped across his. Their panthers were just under their skins, begging for the bite to connect them.

Lucky moved slowly, letting her body adjust to his cock. Sofia's legs wrapped around his body, using her heels to dig into his lower back. "You want more?"

"Yes, Lucky," she cried. "My panther wants to bite you so badly."

"I'm not done making love to you," he warned. "They can wait."

Lucky stroked her dark brown hair, cupping her face. They'd known each other all of their lives, but what they were doing made him see Sofia in a different light. He was her mate, and it still shocked him that his mating scent took so long to make itself known.

"I never thought I'd find a mate within my pride, but I'm so thankful to the gods that it was you."

"I feel the same way, Lucky," she said, tears welling up in her eyes. "I've been working so much that I haven't had time to spend with you, or anyone else from the pride, for years. I wanted my own freedoms for a while, but now…now that I know whose mating scent I had recognized…I'm happy. I'm so damn happy you are mine."

Hearing the words roll from her tongue caused his panther to purr. The vibrations from his chest spurred her own animal to call out to him. She was close to her orgasm, and he had to make their connection official.

"On your hands and knees, princess," he ordered, pulling from her body. She whimpered for a moment before scrambling into the mating position. The moment he breached her body again, he cursed loudly when his panther took over.

There was no explaining what happened. There was no sense of time when he locked his hand into her hair, pulling her body to his chest, and there was no hesitation when his canines sank into the spot where her neck and shoulder met.

Her blood spilled across his tongue, and he swallowed it down. When his teeth slid free from her body, she bucked and knocked him over on his back. She cupped his erection and threw her leg over his body, taking him inside her. She rose and fell over him three times before her eyes flashed a glowing amber. In the next heartbeat, Sofia struck, marking him as her own.

They both called out each other's names as their climaxes struck, and Lucky almost blacked out from the release. No matter how many times he'd brought himself to climax while having Sofia's face in his mind, the real thing was a million times better.

And they had all night to continue their mating. Lucky was going to make sure she was fully sated before the clock struck midnight. This was their mating night, and if they were human, it would be the equivalent of their honeymoon. There was also the possibility she would be with child by morning, and Lucky was okay with that. He'd make sure she was cared for every year she was in heat, and if that meant having cubs…he was ready to give them a family.

Chapter 8

It was well past three in the morning when Sofia woke next to her new mate, Lucky. The night before had been perfect and beyond anything she ever thought it would be when finding her mate.

Her heat was gone, and she knew right away they'd created a cub. Her hand rubbed over her flat belly, and she grinned. Twenty-three was young for most shifters to find their mates. Not that it'd never happened, but usually, most of them were older. Finding your mate within your own pride was sort of rare. She'd never dreamed that Lucky Cooper would've become her mate.

But that was okay, because she was happy.

She lay there, watching him sleep. His blond hair was mussed from their love-making, but it didn't distract from how exceptionally handsome he was, and his full lips were parted ever so slightly as he breathed softly in his slumber.

Sofia wanted to wake him…to let him know they'd made a cub together, but she also didn't want to bother him. He was a Guardian, and there would be times he might be needed in a moment's notice. Her mate needed his sleep.

She inhaled deep, catching her own scent. It was a mix of her mating scent and the hormones from a pregnant female. The thought of having a cub every year during her heat made her smile.

There had always been a yearning for a large family, and she wanted that with Lucky. A little part of her mind wondered if he wanted more than one or two cubs, and she prayed he did. She wanted to be a mother, a nurturer to her family, and now she was going to be just that. Her wishes had been fulfilled.

All because of Lucky.

He'd given her the option to touch him, because he was a good male and wouldn't take that away from her by touching her skin. He was a bit dominate, just like all of the Guardians, but he was respectful. That alone would make her fall in love with him. If she wasn't already there.

Love.

Wow.

Love was going to come at some point. It was in their nature to find their mates first, then fall in love as they learned to accept the connection between them. She didn't know why the gods created the shifters that way, but she accepted it.

Wanting to reach out to him, she squeezed her hand into a fist to keep from going through with the desire to stroke the side of his handsome face. Again, it was the middle of the night and she shouldn't wake him.

The surprise he would get when he scented her pregnancy should be left for him when he woke up. Right? Maybe? Gods, she wanted to tell him, but it was more exciting for him to realize it when he woke for the day.

He was supposed to be at the gate to work his shift by seven, but as with all matings, someone would take his place. Talon always had a rule that a newly mated couple could have a few days together without interruptions while they learned about each other and did the whole mating thing.

From what her mother had told her when she came of age, a male would want to lock him and his new mate into their home and not come out for a while, and Sofia was fine with that. Lucky had been quite dominant the night before, but he was also caring. He'd bathed her after they'd made love for hours. He wanted to make sure she was okay because she'd been a virgin.

If she'd had a perfect scenario for mating in her mind, it was amplified by the way Lucky had cared for her and talked her through what they were doing to make the mating official. She reached up and touched the mating mark on her neck. It was dark in the room, but she could feel the two small bumps on her skin from his bite. That alone made her want to wake him up again and make love.

The connection with him was magical in its own right, but their time together was more than that, or at least she thought so. There was never a time where she was worried or scared of what would happen when he breached her untouched virginity. He was careful and put all of his attention on her.

That alone made her fall in love with him even more.

Sofia laid there, dozing on and off for another hour or two before she felt him move. She immediately rolled to her side so she could watch for him to wake. It took another ten minutes before she heard his panther rumble.

She counted to ten, and his eyes popped open. There was a sleepy glaze to his stare, and it took him another second or two before his human nose flared.

"My mate…you made me a cub," he growled, rolling her over to her back as he climbed over her, sliding down her naked body to press his nose to her belly. "My cub! My cub!"

"Yes, Lucky," she breathed. "We made a cub last night."

"Your scent is so strong," he said after taking another deep inhale. "We are going to have a cub!"

He pulled the dark gray sheets up over his body and slid down between her legs, lapping at her aching sex. "I want to devour your taste so it's on my tongue for the rest of the day."

Sofia gasped, but it was followed by a moan.

As soon as the sun was up, Lucky called Harold in a panic. "Sofia is with young. I need you to exam her to make sure everything is okay. I want to make sure my new cub is healthy."

"First of all, congratulations," Harold replied. "Second of all, when did she conceive?"

"Last night," he panted. There was so much excitement running through his veins that Lucky couldn't contain his need to make sure everything was okay with his mate and cub.

"Lucky," Harold said in his doctor's voice. "She just conceived. As long as she isn't bleeding or sick, I can't do an ultrasound for a few more weeks."

"What?" Lucky barked. "But…my cub and mate."

"Are going to be fine," Harold finished his ramblings.

"What do I do?" Lucky asked in desperation.

"Care for her," Harold reminded him. "Let the pregnancy do its thing. Sofia is a young, healthy female. Her body knows what to do, and I can come by if it'll give you some assurance. However, as far as checking the cub, it will have to wait until she is farther along. You must remember that shifters can *scent* a pregnancy right after it happens. Humans wait almost twenty weeks before they have an ultrasound to see the baby."

"Twenty weeks!" he snarled. There was no fucking way he would be waiting twenty damn weeks to check on his cub.

"Yes, twenty weeks," Harold confirmed.

"Fine," Lucky growled. "Please come by after breakfast and give her a physical."

"I'll come by around ten," Harold advised. "Now, Lucky?"

"Yes?"

"If she starts getting sick, it's the pregnancy," Harold began. "Most females have morning sickness in the first three months. Just keep her hydrated and try to get food into her for nutrition."

"I can do that," he replied, trying to tamp down his nerves.

"Crackers," Harold began to tick off on his fingers. "Rice, chicken…proteins."

"Yes, sir," Lucky acknowledged. Trying his best not to panic. He didn't want her to be sick. Sofia was to be cherished and honored. She was *carrying his cub*!

The moment he hung up the phone, a knock sounded on the door. It was a heavy knock and could only belong to one person…a Guardian…her brother.

The moment Lucky opened his door, Savage inhaled deep, and tears built in his eyes. "It's true?"

"It is," Lucky said with a smile and a proud nod. "It really is, Savage."

Lucky

Savage pushed through the door; his eyes set on his sister who was just emerging from the bedroom. Her dark, brown hair was messy around her delicate face.

"Sister?" Savage cheered, scooping her up into a soft hug, and a soft embrace from her brother was almost unheard of. The male was huge and fierce.

"I'm so happy, Sav," she whispered, but Lucky heard her. His mate was happy, and that was all he'd ever wanted in a mate. Knowing they'd made a cub on their first night together was even better.

Savage slapped him on the back, a little harder than usual, and smirked, "You hurt her, I kill you regardless of the Guardian oath. Feel me?"

"I do, Savage," Lucky replied, not even breaking a sweat. "I'll protect her with my life."

"You best do that," his new brother-in-law replied. They laughed quietly as Sofia stood beside them with tears in her eyes.

Savage excused himself and gave Sofia a wink as he closed the door. It was refreshing to have the biggest Guardian not want to kill him for touching his sister, and Lucky laughed out loud as he turned for his new mate. "That went better than I thought."

"He's really a softy, but I didn't tell you that," she chuckled, and placed her hand over her flat stomach.

"So, this is our new forever, huh?" Lucky asked, walking up to his mate, covering her hand with his own.

"It is," she replied with a nod.

He didn't say anything else, pulling her to his broad

chest. He'd dreamed of the day he would find a mate, and it had finally come true. Not only did he find his mate, but she was now carrying his cub.

"We should get you something to eat," he said with a jerk, remembering what the healer had told him. "You need nourishment."

"I feel fine, Lucky," she promised. "Let me make you something instead."

"I can't let you do that," he panicked. There was no fucking way his mate would be slaving over a stove to cook him something while she was carrying his cub. Hell…to…the…no.

"Lucky," she growled, touching the side of his face. Her eyes were flickering between icy blue and amber. "I'm not injured. I'm pregnant. You can't coddle me for the next nine months."

Little did his sweet mate know…he would, in fact, keep her comfortable and protected for the duration of her pregnancy and each day she stood at his side until their gods called them home.

"Well, today, we are going to stay in our mated bed, right after I warm up this cabin," he declared, noticing the fire was dying down.

She released him, and he watched her disappear into their room. He breathed deep and felt the need to follow her. He had to shake off the scent of his pregnant mate and get some wood from the porch or he'd be drunk on it for the next nine months.

Chapter 9

A *bright flash of light* brought Talon to his feet. The sheriff, and the pride's angel protector, didn't miss a step as he came right up to the desk.

"What's wrong, Garrett?" Talon knew the sheriff only flashed in when there was danger on the horizon, and he immediately called out for every available Guardian to come to his office. "And where the hell have you been?"

It'd been a few months since the sheriff had made an appearance, and even though the pride had been living in peace, Talon worried where the male had run off to without a word.

"First of all, I was summoned home," he answered. Garrett's home was in the heavens with the gods, and

Talon had known that time there ran differently than it did on Earth. "Secondly, I know I'm not supposed to have visions of paranormal issues coming your way, but something isn't right with the small pride you just brought into your home. There is more to it than just a rogue pack of wolves destroying almost the entire pride."

"What are you saying? Are these elders and the lone young female a threat to my pride?"

"Not necessarily." Garrett frowned in a way that made his forehead wrinkle while he thought about the things he'd seen. "I have someone getting information for me on the pride and the land they lived on. There had been some money issues with them, and my guy is looking into the possible foreclosure on that land. Did anyone of them tell you about any money or legal problems the alpha may have been facing?"

"No," Talon answered with a shake of his head. "They are all very traumatized, and the young girl, well, she's quiet. I don't know what those wolves did to them, but I have a feeling it wasn't pleasant."

"I don't mean to sound crass," Garrett said with narrowed eyes. "I just want you to look further into their survival from that attack while I figure out what really happened that night when the rogues attacked them."

"Do you think it was related?" Talon pressed.

"I don't want to speculate," Garrett replied, but he raised a brow that told Talon the angel was leaning toward some type of premeditated attack. "Just talk to them…see what they know. If I find any leads, you'll be the first to know."

"I'll call you if I find out anything that might be of help to you," Talon vowed, tapping his hand over his heart in a show of respect and promise.

With a flash, the sheriff disappeared into thin air. Talon had finally become accustomed to the angel's supernatural way of traveling. They were all some sort of otherworldly animal slash creatures anyway. What the gods did with their angels was above Talon's source of knowledge, and to be honest…he didn't want to know the details of the sheriff's secrets. As much as he hated the male when he was trying to mate Liberty, Talon had finally accepted the sheriff's help in keeping them safe.

Now, he had to figure out why the angel came to him with paranormal issues when the gods had sent him to the pride to protect them from humans.

Something didn't sit right in the alpha's gut, and the moment Guardians started piling in his office, they immediately knew there was something going on that would put them all on edge until the threat was destroyed.

"Come in," Talon ordered. "We might have a problem on our hands."

Lucky was the second one to arrive, and Talon jerked his head to the side to get the male's attention. While the other Guardians were finding their places, Talon whispered to one of his youngest Guardians. "Why are you not with your mate?"

"She's sleeping, and your message was full of worry and power," Lucky replied. "I couldn't stay home when the pride needed me."

"That's very thoughtful of you," Talon said with a smile. "However, after this meeting, I'm giving you a few days off to care for your mate and new cub."

"Thank you, alpha." Lucky nodded and returned to his spot by the door. "If you need me, I will be there to help protect the pride."

"And that is exactly why I chose you to be one of my Guardians," Talon vowed with a heartfelt smile. "Take care of your mate."

As the voices dissipated, Talon began telling them all what the sheriff had said. There was a rumble around the room, and it was expected. If there was a threat to the pride, and from the sound of it coming out of the angel's mouth, the Guardians and Protectors would be on edge until everyone received answers to the newest threat.

"Please bring the new members to my office," Talon ordered a few of the males. It was time to talk to them to find out exactly what happened at their old pride.

He wouldn't let harm come to his family. Whatever happened that night with the wolves just didn't add up.

Sofia slapped at the handle of the toilet in Lucky's bathroom. It was only the first day of being pregnant, and her body wasn't happy. Anything she'd tried to eat, even

Lucky

crackers, was coming back up with the water she'd had to rehydrate her pregnant body.

Touching her stomach, she felt the tears pool in her eyes. She'd found her mate during the worst time for a female shifter. The heat was excruciating, and she was a little jealous of the females who were changed and not born. They had it a lot easier.

She'd just brushed her teeth when she heard the front door to Lucky's cabin open and his deep voice call out for her. "Sofia? Where are you?"

"In here!" She hurried along to change her clothes, knowing if he'd found her hovering over the toilet, he would worry.

His heavy footsteps echoed on the hardwood floors as he made his way to the bathroom. She straightened her features and turned toward the handsome male when he pushed the door open. "Everything okay?"

"I'm fine," she promised him, but she wasn't the best liar. Her brother, Savage, always knew when she was full of shit, and from the narrowed eyes of her mate, he knew it too.

"Are you sick?"

Sofia took a deep breath and nodded her head. Ugh! She hated that her face gave away her lies. "Just a little."

"Why didn't you call me?" he growled low in his throat as his eyes flashed amber sparks.

"You were in a meeting with the alpha," she huffed and shook her head. "I would never interrupt that."

"Princess," he whispered, gently reaching for her

side. His eyes scanned her body a second before pulling her to his chest. "You are my mate, and if you needed me, I would be here in a second. Our alpha knows the importance of a newly mated couple who has a cub on the way. Talon would catch me up on the meeting. So, from now on…don't ever hide anything from me."

"Okay." Sofia melted into his arms, resting her head on his chest. They stood there for several minutes before her stomach growled. "You're right. Talon took days off with each of Liberty's pregnancies. I should've realized that."

"Let me feed you," he said after kissing her forehead. "Tell me what you are craving so I can make you something that will be easy on your stomach."

"Chicken," she hummed. "Something with chicken."

She didn't realize how hungry she was until he asked. She'd expelled everything she'd tried to eat while he was gone, and it was best for the cub if she had plenty of protein.

"Go lay on the couch, and I'll make you some chicken soup," he pressed, pulling her by the hand and directing her to the living room.

"Heavy on the chicken," she called out, smiling when he gave her a thumbs up over his shoulder on his way to the kitchen.

She wasn't going to argue with him, because she was exhausted. It was only ten in the morning, but she knew how pregnant females dealt with being with young. She'd seen it many times over the years with the alpha's mate, Liberty, and her brother's mate, Mary Grace. The first three months were going to be the hardest.

"I have your food simmering," he announced. "Rest until it's ready."

Lucky pulled a blanket from the back of the couch and ordered her to lay down. The moment the blanket came to rest over her body, she sighed heavily and closed her eyes. A little nap was in order as the only sound in the cabin was the pop and crackle of the fireplace and the rustling of pots and bowls in the kitchen.

With her hand over her still flat abdomen, Sofia relaxed while she waited for her new mate to care for her and bring her nourishment. Usually, the females were the ones to cook and care for the males, and she'd be lying if she said it wasn't nice to have Lucky do things for her. She needed it, and as her eyes fluttered closed from exhaustion, she smiled into the pillow under her head.

Malaki rounded up the new pride members and walked them over to the main house, explaining how Talon wanted a meeting with them. The young female, Cheyenne, stuck close to his side as they walked, but she didn't speak or touch him. He could feel her body's warmth as she walked, and he wondered what had happened to make her so quiet. There was a time for answers, but it wasn't his position to ask. That information belonged to his alpha, and if there was a threat like the sheriff had pointed out, he would eventually know.

The elders followed them inside, and after Malaki had knocked on Talon's office door, he held it open until the last female had entered. His alpha gave him a knowing nod and a silent message to stand outside the door unless he was needed.

Yes, alpha.

Malaki replied to Talon and took his post outside the office. It didn't matter that he wasn't actually in the room. His supernatural hearing caught everything that was said.

There were questions about their old pride, and the elders answered everything honestly. Even outside the room, Malaki's senses were strong enough to scent a lie. However, the female, Cheyenne, never talked. She stayed silent, and that bothered him.

What was her secret? Who had hurt her so badly that she never spoke unless it was necessary?

A foreign feeling punched him in the heart. If he thought about the female, which he had over the last few hours, she was really like him.

Broken.

Scared.

Angry.

Oh, the anger. His panther could sense her pain, too. It was like a vinegary scent around her. He knew that all too well. He'd had his own trauma, but what about the female?

What did those wolves do to her?

He had to control his anger at her past, and he couldn't understand why his panther was so…angry at the knowledge. With the female inside the alpha's office, it didn't give him any sense of peace. He wanted to know everything.

As his mind churned over the possibilities, he felt a weird stirring in his chest.

"Malaki?" she spoke up as she exited Talon's office, but it was so soft he would've missed it if his mind wasn't on her past.

"Yes, Cheyenne?"

"Are we in trouble?" she asked, her hands shaking as she rubbed her palms together.

"No, sweetheart," he mumbled. "Our…your alpha just has questions about your old pride's land. There is nothing to worry about. I promise you."

Malaki was shocked at his soft words for the female. Something about her fear made him want to protect her, and it was nothing like the need to protect his pride mates.

No, this was different.

Chapter 10

Talon sat in his office chair, resting his elbows on the old wooden desk that belonged to his late father. The five new pride members sat before him with fear in their eyes.

"I do not want any of you to be afraid of me," he began, leveling his eyes on the two brothers to the old Patton alpha. "I understand your brother was the leader of your old pride?"

His question was met with nods.

"We've gotten word there might have been some problems with the land he owned. Do you know anything about that?"

"My brother never told us anything regarding pride business," Ellington spoke up. "We were never picked as

Guardians when we were younger, and since the pride was left to Alan, we never questioned his business, nor did we ever go against any of his orders. He was our alpha for a long time."

"Alan was a great alpha," Gianna Love, one of the elder females who'd been brought to the pride, blurted. "Our life there was simple, and we were a happy pride. That was…until the wolves showed up."

"When did they arrive?" Talon pressed. He needed answers. There was something not right about the finances of their pride and the sudden appearance of the wolves.

"I'd scented wolves about ten days before they attacked us," Hurley, the other alpha's brother, admitted. "When I went to Alan to advise him, he told me to leave it alone, because the Guardians of our pride would protect us."

"As you know, that didn't happen," Ella Love, the other elder female, said with a soft curse under her breath. "They came in the middle of the night…even had keys to get into each cabin if it was locked. The wolves took the males first, and…and they killed them at the solstice circle where we would gather every season."

Ella, the younger of the two females, burst into tears. When Talon glanced at the young female, she was shaking where she stood behind Ella, squeezing her shoulder for support. The young female was scared out of her mind, and since they'd all taken Talon's blood, he could *feel* their fear.

"Cheyenne," Talon addressed. "Who were you related to in your old pride?"

"Just the caregivers, sir," she paused to swallow. "My mother, Annabelle, was the cubs' caregiver while the Guardians worked. I was working with her when they came in…"

Cheyenne sucked in a breath that sounded more like she was gasping for air. It didn't take Talon long to realize that the young female was in shock from the things she'd seen.

"I know it's very hard for you to talk about, and I can only imagine the things you've seen," Talon said, pushing out a calming power toward all five of them. "Word has reached us that your old alpha may have been in financial trouble. Do any of you know anything about that?"

All of them, except Cheyenne, frowned. The two brothers shook their heads and denied any knowledge, and so did the two elder females. But Cheyenne looked at her feet.

"Is there something you should be telling me, Cheyenne?" Talon pressed her. He was a fair alpha, and would always give his pride a chance to tell him what he wanted to know without forcing his powers upon them, but with the young female, he knew he would have to break his rule.

He tucked his chin and pulled upon his alpha powers, directing them toward the female. "Cheyenne? Would you like the others to leave?"

The young redhead paused, searching the eyes of her elder pride mates. The females gave her nods of encouragement while the males, and brothers to their old alpha, looked on in confusion.

"Tell Alpha Shaw," Gianna urged. "You can't keep what you've seen to yourself. Here, sweetheart, sit in my seat." Gianna raised from her chair, offering it to the female. She hugged Cheyenne and whispered words of encouragement before letting her go.

Once Cheyenne was in her seat, she took a deep breath and looked toward Talon. There were tears in her eyes as she told her story.

"Alpha Shaw, I was in the main house with my mother when the wolves arrived," she admitted. "They rushed the house and started fighting our Guardians. They used knives. Direct hits to the hearts like they'd been trained. I tried to protect the children, locking and hiding them in the daycare room, but the wolves heard the cubs crying and came for us."

Talon held up his hand, steadying himself for what he knew was coming next. "You don't have to continue if you don't want to, Cheyenne."

"I heard them talking to our alpha right before they came into the room," she cried. "They were forcing him to sign over the land to them, but he refused, saying that they were already too late. They'd waited too long to take over the mortgage. The bank had already started the foreclosure."

"So, your alpha was trying to sell the land to the

wolves?" Talon growled out his question.

"I believe so," she nodded. "One of the cubs cried out in fear, and one of the wolves came for us. I was in there...and...and...I saw it all. They killed the cubs. They tried to kill me."

"What did you do to survive?" Talon pressed.

"My father, before he died, taught me many things about protection, and one of them was if I was ever hurt to play dead until the threat was gone," she explained with more tears falling over her cheeks. "He told me that sometimes you can't win, but you can always outsmart the enemy. I was bleeding from my chest after one of them stabbed me. I fell to the ground and pretended to be dead. They didn't even care to check to make sure I was, in fact, dead. After that, they rushed the pride. Gianna and Ella were shoved into a storm shelter under their house by their mates, and Ellington and Hurley ran for the woods. I feel so guilty that I couldn't save the children, alpha. So...guilty. I had to lay there with my eyes open as if I was truly dead so I could see if they came back for me, and in doing so, I saw them...all of the children..."

"That's enough, Cheyenne," Talon ordered, coming around his desk to comfort her. The moment he sent out a healing and calming order to her and the elders, Talon's beast wanted to roar to the skies.

No one should've seen the things they'd seen. Especially this young female.

"Shh, now, Cheyenne," he cooed. "It's over. You're

safe here, and I promise you that our Guardians won't ever let a pack of wolves get on our land."

"It wasn't just the wolves," she continued to cry. "Our alpha...the one male who'd promised to care for us...sold us out, promising the wolves they could own our homes...our lands."

The four elders gasped at her words. It was obvious no one knew what Cheyenne had heard, nor did they know the alpha to the Patton pride was behind the killing of their people.

"Cheyenne, I need to ask...what is your last name?" Talon had no idea who this young female was, and she'd refused to tell anyone how she was connected to the pride, but Talon had an idea.

"My name is Cheyenne Nichols, and Alan Patton was my grandfather," she finally admitted. "My mother was his youngest daughter, and he made sure she was killed before the wolves turned on him and took his life, too."

"So far so good," *Harold* laughed as he put away his ultrasound machine. The hum in the room was making Sofia sleepy, and all she wanted to do was eat a meal she may or may not be able to hold down before it was time to retire for the evening.

Thankfully, the snow was gone, and the weather was a little warmer than it had been a couple of weeks ago.

Lucky

The sun was out all day, but the pride had been quiet, for the most part. From the whispers amongst the other pride members, Talon was in talks with the newest arrivals, trying to get information on their old pride.

Lucky was ordered to be off for the next few days to care for Sofia, but she thought it was unnecessary because she was fine, and with the extra check-up from the healer, she was certain her new mate could go back to work as soon as possible. All she wanted to do was sleep anyway.

"Let's get you home and have some dinner," Lucky offered.

He was a younger version of his brother, Storm, with his blond hair and icy blue eyes, but he was also different. He didn't fight their mating like Storm had done with his mate, Amaya. No, Lucky embraced her and their connection after a short bout of uncertainty over her friendship with Malaki.

It bothered her she hadn't seen him since the night she went into heat. She also appreciated his respect when it came to mating Lucky. Malaki was a walking timebomb most of the time, and she was thankful he hadn't exploded when he realized they were going to mate.

But she'd be lying if she said she didn't miss her friend.

She *did* miss him, terribly.

"The sun is out, but the weather is going to change again," Lucky announced as he entered his cabin with an armful of cut wood. "Temps will be in the teens tonight."

"Can we go to my cabin to gather a few things?" she blurted. If it was going to be cold, she wanted her favorite pair of fuzzy socks and pajamas even though sleeping in Lucky's oversized shirts hadn't been too much of a problem. She loved his scent, but she still longed for her own clothes.

"Of course." He nodded with a smile. "Are you wanting to move in with me anytime soon?"

She paused for a moment, "I hadn't even thought of that, Lucky."

"You are my mate, Sofia," he mentioned.

"I know," she sighed. "It's happened so fast. I…I just can't wrap my head around everything."

"Hey," he sobered, dropping the logs by the wood stove before coming to her side. "Every mating is different, and obviously ours is not quite like some of the other matings in our pride. There is a lot we need to discuss, and I promise to give you space if you need it, but I don't want you to leave. I like having you here."

"Then, there is the discussion about my cabin," she added.

"Yes, about that," he replied, and she knew he was trying not to snarl, because her cabin actually belonged to Malaki. Her friend had gifted it to her, but it was rightfully his.

"I need to see him," she admitted after a moment of silence. "He needs to know he doesn't have to live in the dorms when I move in with you."

Lucky

"So, you are moving in with me?"

"Yes," she said. "Lucky, our nature doesn't lie, and I know I have strong feelings for you. We have a cub on the way. I think we should use the next nine months to explore where this mating is going."

"But first, you need to talk to Malaki," he finished for her.

"I do," she agreed, placing a hand over his heart. "I also need to do it on my own. You two haven't been the best of friends over the years. I don't want you, or Malaki for that matter, to lose your tempers around me."

"I don't like him," he stated.

"He doesn't like you, either," she chuckled. "No hard feelings there, but you know it's the truth."

"I get it," he replied, rubbing his temple. "I really do. I just don't want him to upset you."

"He won't," she promised.

"I trust you, Sofia," Lucky vowed. "Go, see him, but if you return to me harmed or in tears, I *will* kill him."

"There won't be any murders," she replied. "Let me contact him and see if we can meet up tomorrow. Is that okay with you?"

"Why are you asking me for permission? It's not only his house, it's yours too."

"I'm not asking for permission." She paused, reaching for his cheek where she rested her palm against it. "You are my mate, and I know you will be worried. I just want you to not go feral because I'm talking to your enemy."

Sofia watched as her mate's eyes softened. He leaned over and pressed his lips to hers before moving them to her forehead. "I trust you to return to me unscathed."

"Thank you, Lucky," she breathed out and pressed her body against his, feeling the mating connection as they stood there for the longest time.

"I don't think you need to worry about going to see him," Lucky said when his body stiffened. Her mate had a direct line of sight to the front of his cabin through the window, and when Sofia turned around, she saw Malaki step onto the porch.

She didn't wait for him to knock before she rushed over to open the door. "Mal?"

"Sofia," he greeted, looking over her shoulder. "Lucky."

"What are you doing here?" she asked, covering her mouth as soon as the harsh words left her lips. "I'm sorry. That was rude."

"I didn't take it as rude," he replied with a rare smile.

"Would you like to come inside?" Lucky asked as he came to Sofia's back. "I think we all need to talk."

Malaki watched Lucky, who was watching Sofia. There was tension between all of them. Sofia felt it. She could even scent the fear on her tongue.

"If you don't mind," Malaki replied.

"Okay. Enough with this." Sofia blurted. "Mal, come inside. Have a seat and let's talk this out. I don't

Lucky

want any fighting, and I sure as hell don't want my mate and my best friend to hate each other."

Both of the males stared at her in shock for several seconds. Of course, Sofia was the soft-spoken little sister to the strongest Guardian of the Shaw pride, but she wasn't going to let the two males in her life go to blows because they didn't like each other.

It was time for that to stop, and she was going to be the one to put their hatred of each other to rest.

Lucky's cock was hard as stone as his mate took charge of the differences between the two males she had feelings for. At one point, he was certain Sofia would take Malaki as a mate even if they were not destined. It didn't take long for her to realize that Lucky was, in fact, the lucky one who would be her mate for eternity, and now, she was carrying his cub.

"Look, I'm not here to cause problems," Malaki said the moment he sat at the kitchen table. "I just came by to tell you congratulations, and I've already heard that you two will be graced with a cub."

"This is true," Lucky admitted, sitting across from his mate's closest friend. "There are a lot of reasons why I have a hard time with you being around here, but you've changed since you returned from Louisiana. Whatever happened there, I think it was the best thing for you, and I have to suck up the resentment from our youth to welcome you back."

"That's kind of you, Lucky," Sofia said after she wiped away a tear. Lucky watched as his mate came to his side. Her eyes were on Malaki, but she squeezed Lucky's shoulder before she spoke.

"Mal, I know we've had a history, and I hope that you and Lucky can become friends," she started. "Both of you are very important to me."

"You are very important to me, too," Malaki said, moving his gaze from hers to Lucky. "I want you to know that I had no intentions of trying to mate Sofia. Regardless of my upbringing and my complete lack of regard for anyone in this pride during the time I was a teenager, I still love her as a friend. I guess what I've come here to tell you is that I am happy for you both. If there was any male in this pride I'd hoped would have her hand, it would be you."

Sofia gasped and started to move toward Malaki, but she stopped herself, "Are you leaving again?"

"No," he said. "I need to right a lot of wrongs with members of this pride, and my first stop was here. Lucky and I only got along when we were working together to fight the drug trade and to care for the pride. I've changed since I left, and I know it's going to be hard for the pride to accept me again. I have things I need to work on, and I'm willing to do what I can to make everyone trust me again. I came back because I wanted a life with my sister. Talon has offered me a spot here, but anything I do is going to be subject to scrutiny. I accept that."

"Oh, Mal," she cried.

"It's okay, Sofia," he promised, patting his chest as a sign of respect. "I'm on probation for a few months, but I think everything will work out."

"It will work out, Mal," she enthused. "You are an amazing Guardian, and someday, you'll find your forever."

"You've always had such faith in me, Sofia," he admitted with a soft smile. "I'm very happy for you and Lucky. I hope that I am here for a long to time watch your cubs grow up to follow their father's footsteps to protect the pride."

Lucky couldn't believe what he was seeing and hearing. Malaki had grown into a male of worth since he'd left the pride. He wasn't sure if it was his work with the other pride to stop the wolves or if it was just age. Maybe he had needed the time away from the Shaw pride to work through his anger at the things he'd seen with Calla.

"Thank you, Malaki," Lucky said as he stood to hold out his hand to the male. "I'm glad you've come back. I know your sister has missed you terribly."

"I know she has." He nodded, looking at his watch. "Speaking of Calla…I'm running late for dinner with her and Taze. If you'll excuse me."

They said their goodbyes, and while their conversation was short, Sofia felt better. All she'd ever wanted was for Malaki to fit in, and now that he'd experienced life outside of the Shaw pride, he might just be ready to move on with his life.

Chapter 11

*T*alon watched as *Sofia's car* made its way down the driveway and off the pride's land. He didn't realize she would be heading back into work this soon after her mating with Lucky. Savage's baby sister had turned into a wonderful female, and she was determined to keep her job at the animal clinic and her independence.

A flash of light caught his attention, seeing the angel show up in his regular street clothes and not his uniform.

"Have you found anything?" Garrett asked.

Talon had searched file after file and website after website to find any information on the Patton pride going into foreclosure on their lands, but for the last two weeks, he was at a loss. The newest pride members were of no help, either. They weren't privy to any financials of their pride, and rightly so. It was the alpha's job to make sure his people were cared for in all ways, and that meant keeping their pride lands from being torn away due to negligence.

Garrett paced in front of his desk while rubbing his temples. Even the angel couldn't figure out the relation between the wolves and the pride, but they both knew something was amiss.

"There has to be some lead on their financials, but I have hit a roadblock," Talon cursed, as he stood to look out his office window. "They've done a great job of hiding themselves like most shifters do, but this is just unreal."

"There must be a connection between the pride and those wolves," Garrett barked, coming to stand next to the alpha's chair. "I can't find a connection, and my visions are not helping."

"Should I send a team back to their lands?"

"That might be a good idea," Garrett said. "If those wolves killed the family to take over their property, I bet they've moved in already."

"It might be best to send a few Guardians to watch the place for the night to see what activity is going on," Talon wondered out loud. "If they're causing problems in that area, we need to stop it before they start changing humans and bulking up their numbers."

"I agree," the angel nodded. "I'll go with them, too. I know the sheriff a few towns over. Maybe he could be of use to us."

Lucky

"Have you had any visions?"

"None since I first came to you." Garrett cursed and took a seat in front of the desk. He swayed a little and rubbed his eyes like he was exhausted. Talon knew exactly how he felt. "I know I'm not human, but this nonsense gives me a headache."

"We will figure it...Garrett?"

The angel slumped in his chair...his eyes unfocused and glassed over. Talon used his super speed to come to his side, grabbing the sheriff by the shoulders and shaking him over and over again while calling his name.

"Garrett! Wake up!" he barked, sending out a call to Winter and Savage. Thankfully, his best Guardians weren't far and burst through the office door within a minute.

"What the fuck is going on?" Savage barked as he reached for the angel. "Is he having a vision?"

Once Talon realized what was happening, he moved away from Garrett, waiting until he came out of whatever he was seeing.

Savage and Winter stood protectively at Talon's side, and he could feel the worry coming from his Guardians. Whatever he was seeing could mean trouble for the pride.

With a gasp, Garrett jerked in his chair. His eyes refocused and they flashed white.

"Garrett? What did you see?" Talon ordered, his panther clawing to get out.

"Who's pregnant?" he asked, coming to his feet.

"Who is with child? Tell me!"

"My sister," Savage snarled; his canines thick in his mouth. "What's going to happen to her? Tell me!"

Talon had to place a hand on Savage, sending him a sense of calm, but it didn't work. The male was pale white and ready to destroy the world.

"Sofia?" Winter asked, coming to Garrett's side. "Her name is Sofia."

"Car wreck," Garrett began to ramble. "Blood…fear…water…pain."

"When?" Talon snarled at the sheriff. He'd just seen her leave for work, and he didn't see Lucky in the car with her either.

Before anyone had a chance to react, Savage was out the door, hollering for his sister's mate.

But it was too late. Talon felt the cry of the female. She was trying to connect with him, but it was faint.

"She's hurt," he said as Garrett pulled out his phone, barking orders to Winter about what type of car she drove, but Talon was trying to see through her mind and figure out where she was so help could be there instantly.

River…hurt…help!

"She crashed into the river! Go! Go!" Talon barked as he sent out a call to every Guardian.

"I'll find her, Talon." Garrett flashed out of the room, and Talon prayed the angel would get there in time.

By the time he reached Winter's truck, Lucky was already flying down the road and off the property. A

Lucky

pregnant female was cherished, and from the looks of his pride, they were in as much of a panic as he felt coming from her.

Lucky's heart was beating out of his chest. When the word came through his connection with the alpha, he'd dropped to his knees where he stood. His mate was hurt. His cub could be hurt as well.

A feral snarl left his lips as his brother yanked him to his feet. "We have to go, brother."

A truck was running, and he didn't even realize who was in the seat when the wheels spun, throwing gravel from the alpha's long driveway. When the truck bounced onto the road, he saw Kraven at the wheel. His fellow Guardian had his long hair up into a bun, enhancing his fierce features. The glow from his changed eyes wasn't hard to miss either.

"Savage is in front of us," Kraven barked. "We are going to find your mate and get her home where she belongs."

"My cub," Lucky snarled. "If my mate and cub are harmed, I will kill whoever did this."

"I'll help," he cursed.

She was only minutes from the pride, but it felt like hours as they raced toward the crash site. The same thing had happened with Evie and other mates many years ago. The only thing that ran through Lucky's mind was that whoever crashed into her was going to take his mate from him.

He wouldn't leave anyone standing when he found them.

Talon was sending out calming powers to him through their bond, but it wasn't helping. Lucky had never been so angry in his life.

"You need to accept your alpha's powers, Lucky," Storm warned. "Don't fight him."

"I need this anger to avenge her," he said through gritted teeth. As it was, his canines were thick in his mouth and his eyes were glowing with the presence of his beast. His hands were starting to shift into claws from his beast. He tightened his hold on the animal, reminding him that when they found Sofia, the claws could harm her. It didn't take long before the feral animal inside him listened and backed off enough to return his fingers to their human state.

"There she is!" Kraven hit the brakes on the truck hard enough to throw Lucky's body forward. Her car was off the side of the road, and its hood and engine were submerged in the river close to the pride's land. He didn't even wait for the tires to stop before he was out the door, rushing to the driver's door, ripping it from the hinges with his super strength.

"Princess, talk to me," he cried, seeing blood coming from her head. The wound had already healed from her enhanced abilities, but her arm was across her belly, protecting their unborn cub. However, it was at an

Lucky

odd angle.

Trucks arrived behind him, and her name was being called by several Guardians. One of them was her brother, and he and the others used their brute strength to pull the car away from the edge of the fast-moving river, but Lucky's only worry was his beautiful mate.

"My ankles," she cried, and when he looked down, a feral snarl left his lips. The floorboard of the car was buckled around her feet. "My arm."

"I need to know where else you are hurt," Lucky asked, reaching in to wrap his arms around her, tucking one under her knees and the other behind her back after slicing through the seatbelt with an extended claw. "Sofia. You have to be honest with me right now. I know you're strong, and I know you can heal quickly, but our cub…and your body is very important. Where does it hurt?"

"Just my arm and ankles," she panicked. "Lucky, I tried…I tried to protect our cub."

"You did an amazing job, Sofia, but we are going to get you to Harold right now," he promised, praying to the gods he wasn't lying to her.

The sun was shining high above, but for all Lucky knew, it was the middle of the night. Time passed in odd phases. He tried to listen to the other Guardians, but his mind was only on his mate. One word passed through his human and animal mind, and he shook it away. Now was not the time to feel love toward his mate. His only thought was her safety.

Theresa Hissong

As it was, there was a lot of blood from various cuts and wounds on her body. He kept his shifted ears on high alert, hearing their cub's heartbeat with every breath he took. Lucky was no healer, but he knew the sound of a healthy heart, and he was thankful to the gods that Sofia was able to protect their unborn child.

"I'm going to pick you up now, Sofia," he advised, tightening his hold. "When I do, I need you to not tighten up. Let me carry the brunt of everything. I vow to get you to the healer with no other damage to you or our cub, princess."

"I trust you, Lucky," she moaned as pain flared in her arm. She touched her broken bone with her one remaining good hand, but Lucky acted quickly and took her from the car.

"Don't you worry, princess," he cooed as he climbed the embankment. "Harold is waiting, and Luna will be there to care for you."

"Okay," she sighed and closed her eyes. "Okay, Lucky. I'm so sorry I scared you."

She was trying to be strong and confident, but somehow, Lucky knew she was panicking on the inside. Was that part of their bond? Their mating bond? If so, that knowledge was strong in his mind and in his heart. He couldn't tell anyone who asked if he loved her yet, but there was a part of him who knew that he would love her. Was that the bond getting stronger? Yes, it was. He was so conflicted as to his feelings toward Sofia with Malaki still around, but he did know that he would go to the ends of the earth to fight for her if he was called to protect her from anything that was thrown at them.

Was that love?

Maybe?

It didn't matter. Sofia was his destined mate, and she was carrying his cub. No matter who she loved, Lucky was going to be in her life no matter what the future held for them.

She was his, and his panther snarled in his head to remind him about their kind and how it didn't matter when they touched, their human side would eventually fall in love. It was written in the stars when they were born that their mates were already out there...somewhere. Lucky closed his eyes and held back tears as Sofia cried out from her injuries.

"I'm going to make sure you and our cub are safe...I promise."

The moment Lucky scooped her up into his arms, everything went away. The pain, the fear...all of it. Gone.

"Our cub," she cried. She'd already checked over her body, and the car was a total loss. Someone had run her off the road, sending her car through a small guardrail, plunging the front end into the Coldwater River. Thank the gods it stopped before the entire vehicle was submerged.

"Harold is waiting for us," Lucky said with a broken sob. "I have to get you back to the pride."

"I hurt, Lucky," she finally admitted.

"Where does it hurt, Sofia?"

"Everywhere," she admitted. Most of her minor injuries would heal. The gashes and bruises would be gone by the time they returned to the pride, but her broken arm and ankles would take more time. She's immediately covered her unborn child when she realized she was going to lose control of her little Toyota, and because of that, the airbag deployed and crushed her arm.

Her panther was working overtime to heal the wounds, but if she knew anything about their kind, there were just some things that wouldn't heal correctly until they were set and repaired by the healer.

When she'd finally come to a stop and the river was rushing over the hood of her car, she tried to climb out, but the damage was too severe to both the car and her body. She couldn't walk due to her ankles being at an unnatural angle and her arm was just hanging there.

"I'm going to vomit," she warned.

Lucky dropped to his knees and turned her head where she could expel her breakfast on the embankment. The vision of what she'd seen done to her body was enough.

"Close your eyes, princess," Lucky advised. He had to know she wasn't doing well with the mental aspect of the wreck.

Lucky

She did as she was told and let him care for her. He was, after all, her mate, and the males were very protective. Savage's voice was a calming presence, but she waved him off when he started asking questions.

"Please, Savage," she begged. "Not now." Her brother was leaning over the passenger seat as the vehicle started to move again. She cried out, but she soon realized the other Guardians were pulling the car away from the rushing water.

"I want to know who did this to you!" Savage was angry, and rightly so.

"I was hit by another car...a big, blue truck. I didn't even see the faces of the people inside it."

"I need to move her to the pride, Savage," Lucky snarled. "Questions can be answered *after* I make sure my mate and cub are okay."

Sofia closed her eyes again, turning her head into Lucky's chest. She sobbed while he held her on the drive back to the pride. She didn't even know who was at the wheel, and at the moment, she didn't care.

"I tried to protect our cub," she whimpered. "I covered my belly. That's how I broke my arm." She sucked in a deep breath when the pain flared.

"I know it hurts, princess, and I'll get you some relief in less than five minutes. We are pulling up to the pride now."

The drive up to the healer's cabin was bumpy across the gravel road. Whoever was driving didn't care what speed he was barreling up the road at. The moment the door opened and cold air hit her face, she sighed in relief.

The healer's voice was as calm as a doctor's should be. He had Lucky take her into his operating suite, and she knew then that her injuries would require surgery. Her supernatural healing wasn't going to save her this time.

"Sofia?" Harold called out. "I'm going to take some x-rays of your arm and ankles. We will probably need to set them, and that's going to mean surgery. I have the correct drugs to do that, and I promise you, they won't harm your cub. However, I need to do an ultrasound before we set those bones. I'm going to give you something to help with the pain while we check on your unborn child."

All she could do was nod. Her eyes were fixed on Lucky, but she cried out when five of the Guardians entered the room. She knew what was happening.

"Don't leave me," she begged with tears rolling over her lashes.

"It's for the best that he sits outside," Harold reminded her. "He won't be far."

Lucky started to resist, but Savage and Kraven took him by the arm. Savage whispered something to her mate, and he finally gave in. She already knew that he was on the verge of going feral at seeing her broken and bleeding on the healer's gurney.

"I'll be right outside," he choked. She knew he wanted to say more, but her brother and the other Guardian pulled him away from the room, closing the

Lucky

door as they left. There was a snarl echoing as they left.

Tears formed in her eyes, and Harold was there to give her strength. "My gloves are on, and I will not touch you in a way to bring you any more pain than you are already in."

"Thank you, sir," she said through gritted teeth.

"I want to give you a mild sedative to help with the pain, but I need to check on your cub before I take you into surgery."

On her nod, he produced a syringe from the little metal tray behind him. She didn't even flinch when he injected the medicine into her vein. Two seconds later, Harold's mate, Luna, was there to start an IV. The healer's mate stroked the side of her face with tears in her eyes and leaned over to whisper in her ear, "Everything is going to be okay. I've called your parents. They are outside with your mate."

"Thank you," she slurred as the sedative began to work.

Warm gel spread across her skin below her belly button, and she vaguely remembered the wand rubbing over her body. The swishing sound of the cub's heartbeat lulled her to sleep.

"Sofia," Harold called out her name. When she blinked, he was smiling. "Your cub is healthy. I'm going to get you into surgery to fix that arm and your ankles. After we wake you up, I'll have your mate take you outside to shift. It's going to be a long day and night, but if you do as I ask, you're going to be just fine."

"And my cub?" she mumbled.

"Your cub is nestled inside you, and there are no injuries to your womb," he promised. "You protected him, or her, perfectly."

It wasn't until she heard her cub was safe that Sofia closed her eyes and let the healer do his job. When she woke again, she was groggy, trying to make out sounds in the room. The clink of a metal tray was the loudest, but the closest sound was a soft purr from her mate.

"Lucky…you're here," she whispered, trying to shake off the effects of the medicine.

"I wouldn't be anywhere else, Sofia," he cooed.

"I need to shift," she blurted as her animal pushed to the surface. Her canines thickened and her nose recessed in her face. The shift was upon her, but there were also bandages and an IV in her arm. "Help me, please."

Lucky glanced over his shoulder, and Sofia followed his gaze. The healer gave her mate a nod and stepped out of the room. The walnut-colored door closed and gave her a barrier between the other pride members and her mate. There was something about Lucky that was quickly making her fall in love with him, and it was nothing like her love for her friend, Malaki.

No, this was different…this was *real*.

"I'm going to have to carry you," he told her. "The healer had to put screws into some of your bones, and while they will heal, they're going to have to stay."

"It was that bad, huh?" she asked, trying to sit up on her own, but the pain in her right arm stopped her from

Lucky

moving.

"Don't move," he growled. "Let me care for you. I'm going to be as gentle as possible, and I want you to tell me if anything hurts."

"I trust you," she vowed. The vow of love was on the tip of her tongue, but she swallowed it down. There would be a time and place for that later.

Her mate's arms slid behind her shoulders and the back of her knees. With a gentle movement, she was in his arms, resting against his chest. "Are you hurting?"

"No, Lucky," she promised, breathing in his mating scent. "I'm fine. I just want to let my panther free."

"You can shift while I carry you," he offered, looking down at her body. "The gown Luna put you in has snaps at the shoulders where I can free your panther easily."

With his approval, her panther began the shift. At no time did Lucky stumble when her panther burst through her skin. The animal felt a bit trapped by the gown, but her mate was there to rip it away. She purred and rubbed her snout against his neck, and his own panther made a noise deep in his human throat.

"I'm going to put you down gently," he advised, and did as he'd vowed.

For the next few hours, she would shift between her human and animal, and each time, Lucky was there to cover her human body with a thick blanket to ward off the cold ground beneath her naked body. She didn't know if it'd been hours or minutes before she was finally able to move her right arm and both of her ankles with minimal pain.

"One more shift, princess," he urged.

"So…tired," she mumbled, closing her eyes.

"One more," he pressed. "After that, I will take you home and let you sleep for as long as you need."

"Shift…okay," she mumbled and let her panther take over.

After five minutes, her animal gave up, knowing her body was healed. The moment she became human again, Lucky lifted her and walked out of the healer's backyard, carrying her bundled up in the blanket.

She knew other Guardians were there, but she couldn't focus in on their faces. Sofia was certain her brother was one of them, but he didn't interfere with her mate, and she was thankful he didn't cause a problem. Savage was known to be outspoken, but for some reason, he'd been nothing but inviting to her new mate.

However, she scented Malaki as they walked. The male didn't speak or stop Lucky. Maybe everything was going to be okay between her new mate and the male she considered her best friend…for real this time.

Sofia remembered the bath Lucky had drawn for her, and she even remembered him dressing her in his oversized shirt, but it wasn't until morning that she woke up and got her mind straight from the drugs the healer had given her to perform the surgery to start the healing process of her broken bones.

The one thing she remembered, and the one thing

she would always cherish, was that no matter what happened the night before, Lucky's scent was always right in front of her.

Chapter 12

Malaki and Kraven parked at a church not far from the old Patton pride. Their job was to scope out the land to see if the pack had taken over the land, making it their own.

The moment they arrived, the sun had just set, casting the land in almost total darkness. If it wasn't for the two light poles on the main drive and over the large house on the hill, they would've had to shift to see what was transpiring.

"I see six in the downstairs window," Kraven growled. Hope's brother was a quiet Guardian, but it never fooled Malaki. Even as a teenager, he knew the male was a force, and he was very protective.

"I see two out by the barn," Malaki added.

His panther scratched at his skin, knowing this pack

had done the unthinkable, and that the young female, Cheyenne, had witnessed things she should've never seen at any point in her life. Granted, she was barely over the age of twenty, and she was strong, but there was a fear in her eyes that shook Malaki to his core. No female should be subjected to the things she saw.

As soon as Malaki identified the wolf who'd killed those cubs, he would make the son of a bitch pay with flesh and blood. Talon was angry enough to allow it, too. His orders were to destroy the wolves at any cost, and Malaki was going to relish at the moment he was able to spill the blood of the one who'd murdered those children.

"Have you heard about Sofia?" Kraven asked as they took their spots behind a cluster of trees and shrubs where they could stakeout the land belonging to the old Patton pride. "Has she healed?"

"Yes, I saw her mate taking her home right before we left," Malaki admitted. Talon had given the order for the two of them to go, but Malaki wanted to make sure his friend had healed and that her cub was unharmed. Lucky hadn't seen him standing amongst the other Guardians as he took Sofia back to his cabin, but from the scent coming from Sofia, she was going to be okay. There was no more blood or injuries as far as he knew. Her mate was calm, and not even the slightest bit feral. That was a good sign.

"Good," Kraven cursed. "I want to know if her accident was related to the Patton pride, because if these wolves have knowledge there were survivors, they'll come looking to take them out."

"Not before we destroy them," Malaki vowed. No one would touch the elders or Cheyenne as long as he had life in his body.

"Agreed." Kraven nodded and made himself comfortable. "We have enough food to last us twenty-four hours. Once daylight breaks, we will watch them. One of us should stay here if the wolves leave. The other one needs to take the truck and follow them."

"I'll follow them," Malaki offered, knowing if any of the wolves got close to the Shaw pride, he would die trying to destroy the pack himself.

"Deal," Kraven said, narrowing his eyes on the main house just off the winding road five miles from the main interstate.

As they watched and waited, Malaki scanned the area, taking note of each vehicle parked close to the main house. Two trucks, both white Chevrolets, and a nice, blue truck. As his eyes narrowed, he noticed a dent in the front bumper. There was a scuff within the dent, and he cursed when he saw the color.

Red.

The same color as Sofia's car.

"Kraven," he choked out, trying to keep his animal from making an appearance. As it was, his canines thickened in his human mouth. "I think I know who ran Sofia off the road."

Kraven picked up his phone, dialing the alpha's

number. Since the wolves were nestled into their stolen home, there was no need to partially shift and call out to their alpha.

Malaki stayed focused on the home while he listened to Kraven's discussion with Talon. There was an urgency there, knowing the one group who wanted all other shifters dead had been the ones to harm a pregnant female of their pride.

From the growl Malaki heard through Kraven's phone, he knew things were about to change. The moment his partner hung up, Malaki knew there was going to be a new fight on the horizon, and when he glanced at his watch, he realized it would be happening just as the sun broke across the horizon.

"Talon is sending back up," Kraven whispered. "Let's take turns getting some sleep."

Word had come that the sheriff had a vision only seconds before the accident, and he wondered why he hadn't seen it coming sooner. Could it have been because the accident was a true accident? Or did the person who ran her off the road make a last-minute decision to ram into her car?

Whatever the reason, he was thankful she didn't die.

Which brought up a whole new set of questions. Was the person who hit her a human or a shifter? Or…something else?

The sheriff wasn't always forthcoming with his abilities, and even though he was privy to what exactly the angel's role in helping the pride was, he always

Lucky

wondered if he kept things to himself.

As far as he could remember, the sheriff was *only* there to protect them from human threats, but if the one who'd run her off the road was a part of the pack who'd killed the elders and Cheyenne's family, why did he get that vision?

Were the tasks from the gods changing? Did they change while he was away? What did he miss?

At that point, Malaki didn't care. There was an issue with wolves, and he hated them with a passion. If anyone knew his history, they'd never question his actions when taking those motherfuckers out.

"Son of a bitch!" Kraven roared in the confines of the truck, jolting Malaki out of his sleep. "They're leaving, and fast. Look!"

Sure enough, the wolves were piling into the vehicles, squealing tires as they turned north on the road leading from the Patton pride's home.

"They must've caught our scent," Kraven said, slamming his hand on the steering wheel.

"Follow them," Malaki growled. "See where they go."

"Call Axel or Diesel. Let them know our location." Kraven waited until the cars were just far enough away that he could turn on his headlights and follow them. No matter what spooked the wolves, Malaki knew his partner was keeping their safety at the forefront of his mind.

Malaki called Axel, letting him know what had

happened. "What's your ETA?"

"We are forty minutes behind you," Axel cursed. "Do not engage with them until we catch up."

"I don't know if you'll be able to catch up," Malaki said, looking over at the speedometer. "They are at max speed to get out of that pride house."

"Fuck," Axel bellowed. "We will try and get to you as soon as possible, but keep me informed."

"Will do," Malaki promised and dropped the phone in his coat pocket.

The roar of the engine was the only sound they heard for the next seventy-five miles as the wolves made their way out of town.

Sofia tried to move out from under Lucky's hold as he slept wrapped around her body. She was mostly healed from her injuries, but that didn't mean she wasn't sore. Her enhanced healing had helped her broken bones, but they still gave her discomfort. Thankfully, their cub was safe, and that was all she cared about.

"What's wrong?" Lucky asked as he came awake from her movements.

"Nothing," she promised. "Go back to sleep. It's only four in the morning."

Lucky fell back into his sleep as quickly as he woke. Sofia, however, did not care to close her eyes. She remembered the incident in all its clarity.

Lucky

A blue truck had followed her from where it'd been parked in the lot at The Deuce. Her drive to the office where she worked took about twenty minutes, but the moment she'd turned down an old country road she used as a shortcut, things changed.

The car rode her bumper, and eventually, ran up on her, pushing her off the side of the road. Her heart beat heavily in her chest when she remembered careening down the embankment straight for the river that ran through most of the county.

The river was known for its fast-moving water, and all she could think about was going under while being stuck in her car. Thankfully, she hit the guardrail, slowing her vehicle. If she hadn't hit it, the outcome could've been a lot different.

She may be a shifter with extra healing abilities, but fire, drowning, and a gunshot wound to the head wouldn't be something she could heal from. Thankfully, the car drove off and she was able to call out for help.

*If things had been different...*she shivered, and on instinct, she used her good arm to cover their cub. She was only a few weeks along, but she had a feeling the next eight months were going to be the biggest test of her strength and life. It looked like they were going to have another crisis on their hands.

She swiped at her eyes, removing the tears that began to fall, praying she didn't make a sound to wake up her mate. The last thing she wanted was for Lucky to worry. There was a yearning in her chest...a feeling she'd never experienced. The thought of him going out to defend her honor scared her to death.

If she really dug deep...*really* deep, she would say that there was a bond forming between them beyond the mating connection. Was it love? Could it be that easy?

Maybe it was...

He was her mate, after all.

There were tales of mates throughout their histories that proved the gods, and their essential makeup, was correct. First came the scents...then touch...after that, they would eventually fall in love. She knew her own parents had been like that. Her mother talked fondly about her father touching her by accident and then they worked hard on their relationship...becoming friends first, and within a month or two, they fell in love.

The only difference was that her mother hadn't been in heat the moment they had decided to touch.

Now, Sofia was pregnant.

She was scared.

"What's wrong?" Lucky came awake when she inhaled a little too loudly. Damn it! She didn't want him to worry, but as he turned on the light next to the bed, she saw his amber eyes and knew it was too late.

"I'm...I'm scared, Lucky." Sofia sniffled once and held back the tears.

"I promise you that no one will hurt you again, princess," he said, touching the side of her face. His warmth bled into her, and she started to shake her head. "What is it?"

Lucky

"I'm scared of that, but I'm also scared of us," she admitted, pointing at him and then herself. "I know that I will love you until the day I die, but how we get there…that's what scares me."

"The last thing I would ever do is fail you, Sofia," he gasped, pulling her to his chest. The moment they made contact and their mating bond flared, the hold on her emotions broke and her eyes couldn't hold the tears back any longer.

"I know you won't, and you haven't, but what if I fail you?"

"Fail me?" he balked. "Sofia, you could never fail me."

"How do you know? How do I know? I mean," she paused to catch her breath and look into his eyes. She wanted to see his reaction to her worries. "What if I'm not a good mate? What if we are not compatible?"

"I think we are very compatible," he smirked.

"Not just the sex," she blushed.

"Look," he began, rearranging them so they were sitting on the bed facing each other. He took her tiny hands and rubbed his thumbs over them. "We've known each other all of our lives, right?"

"Yeah." Sofia nodded.

"And we've always gotten along even though we weren't really in the same age group, right?"

That was true. She was only twenty-three and Lucky was twenty-nine. They'd never been close. He'd always hung out with the other males his age, and Sofia kept to herself a lot. Sure, she and Calla had been friends when the female had arrived at the pride, and of course, there was Evie who was a little older than her, but growing up, Sofia was more of an introvert. Yes, she and Lucky had made small talk several times at pride gatherings, and once he gained his Guardian status, he would run with them on the nights of the solstice or equinox pride hunts.

On her nod, he used his finger to lift her chin. "Sofia, I promise to love you one day, and when that day comes, you will know it. You'll never have to question my feelings for you."

"You're making it very easy to fall in love with you, Lucky Cooper," she chuckled and wiped her eyes.

He was different with her. The big Guardian was a force when he was protecting the pride, but when they were alone, she got to see a different side to him.

"Come on, Sofia. Let's sleep," he suggested, sliding down in the bed. "You and our cub have had a long day, and we are both taking the day off."

Chapter 13

Lucky woke a few hours later and watched Sofia sleep, knowing he'd already fallen in love with her. It took him almost losing her for his mind to realize that she was everything he needed in a mate.

She had her reserves, and rightly so. Their kind did things differently, and even though they were raised by their elders to know that the touch was just the beginning, his grandfather had told him once, the love of a true mate could change a male and complete him. He'd do anything for her and move mountains if she asked.

Lucky wanted to move mountains for Sofia and their cub.

He carefully checked his phone and cursed to himself when he saw that Talon had called a meeting that morning, and he'd missed it. After a quick text to Talon, Lucky slid carefully from the bed. She started to stir, but he leaned over to kiss her head.

"Talon called a meeting," he whispered. "Go back to sleep. I'll be home as soon as I can."

She mumbled and rolled over, falling back into her slumber.

It was hard to leave her there alone, but he knew if the alpha had called a last-minute meeting, something was wrong. He hoped it was news on those wolves who'd killed the Patton pride.

"Talon?" Lucky called out and knocked on the frame of the doorway leading into the alpha's office.

"Come on in, Lucky," Talon said after looking up from his computer. "You were not expected to be here this morning, by the way."

"Still," Lucky grimaced. "I've never missed a meeting."

"Sit down," Talon suggested, pointing to a chair. "Let me catch you up on what Malaki and Kraven have been doing."

"Did they find the wolves?" Lucky blurted, feeling his panther pacing in his mind.

"They did, but something spooked the pack just after midnight," Talon said, rubbing his temples. The alpha had dark circles under his eyes. "Malaki and Kraven followed them into Kentucky, and once Axel and Diesel caught up to them, it was too late. I've let Garrett handle getting word to some of his police friends up there. Maybe they can catch them, but we are at a loss. I can't let my Guardians be that far away from the pride. It just isn't safe."

"What do we do now?" Lucky asked, thinking of a million reasons why letting those wolves go was a really bad fucking idea. From the look on his exhausted alpha's face, the leader felt the same way.

"We go back on alert until they are found," Talon ordered. "I hope that they're picked up in Kentucky and we can claim shifter law on them. If we can, and they are brought here, we will end them for what they've done."

"So, you won't send them to Colorado?" Colorado was where the humans who'd been turned and brainwashed by the wolf alphas were given the blood of an alpha who taught them how to live their new lives. Gabriel had given them a second chance at life.

"I'm not ruling that out, but I can't let the murder of innocent children go unpunished."

Lucky tightened his fists on the arms of the chair and nodded. "I agree, alpha."

"What do you mean, I have to quit my job?" Sofia snarled at her mate. Whatever had happened in that meeting with Talon had Lucky pacing the living room floor. He was about to wear a hole in the carpet if he didn't slow down.

"The wolves ran from Kraven and Malaki," he

admitted. "They hit the Kentucky state line and that's when our Guardians lost them. They haven't been found, and we are worried they might come back for the rest of the Patton pride."

"Damn it," she barked. "We had just found peace, and now this!"

"Please, understand that I did not want to tell you this," Lucky said as he took both of her hands into his. "Sofia, it's dangerous again."

"I'm tired of living in fear, Lucky," she cried. "We should've never made ourselves known."

"I agree that things were more peaceful when we were younger, but it was bound to happen one day. Our pride is large, and with the technology humans have, they would've found out about us sooner or later. Talon did the right thing by going forward and stopping the human's fear before it got too bad."

"I know, but still…" She let her sentence die.

"Please, just stay home for a month. Give us that long to find the wolves," he begged, kissing the back of her hand. His mating scent was thick ever since he had walked into his cabin after meeting with Talon. The thicker the scent, the more protective the male was feeling, and she understood that. "My concern is for you and our cub. The thought of you trying to go to work and them returning to hurt you, or anyone else in the pride, scares the living hell out of me."

"I know," she nodded. "It scares me, too."

"So, you'll take some more time off?"

Lucky

"Yes," she finally agreed. "Are we allowed to roam freely on our own land?"

"Yes, for now," he admitted. "Why do you ask?"

"I'd like to go see my brother and his mate today. Will you come with me? I know my parents are going to be over there for dinner. It's time we talk to them about our mating."

"You mean I have to meet your father?" he gulped, making Sofia laugh out loud.

"My father isn't as scary as Savage," she chuckled, raising a brow.

"Your brother's not that scary," he shrugged.

"Well, you haven't made him angry, yet," she retorted.

Sofia laughed some more as Lucky's eyes widened. "I'm going to shower."

"Do you need some help?" he winked.

Sofia shooed him away as she headed for his bathroom, undressing and stepping into the warm water. Her mate was very attentive, and after her breakdown the night before, she felt better. There would be a time when she was deeply in love with him, and she knew it was coming. She was still scared, but with him at her side, she felt safer.

By the time she was out and dried her hair, he returned to the bathroom to take his own shower. She tried not to watch him through the fog-covered doors, but she couldn't resist roaming her eyes over the silhouette of his sculptured body.

Theresa Hissong

He was a Guardian, and one of the strongest males in her pride. He was everything she'd prayed for from the moment she'd turned twenty and had started her adult shifter journey in finding a mate. It took a little longer than she'd hoped, but that was because she was always working, making her own money.

Working for the animal clinic was her best choice for a job. Unlike most shifters, they couldn't be around the dogs or cats because their animal nature scared the humans' companions, but Sofia was a lot softer and not as scary to them. She loved animals of all kinds, even her own species. The fact she had to take time off bothered her, but she knew it was for the best.

She would do as her mate asked and stay home until the wolves were found, and during that time, she thought she'd get her sister-in-law to go over and make friends with the youngest female from the Patton pride.

Cheyenne was living in the old dorms and was probably scared out of her mind. That female had seen things no one, human or shifter, should ever witness.

Sofia had an idea and voiced it to Lucky after he dried off and changed into clean clothes.

"Why don't you call Hope and Evie, too?" he suggested.

"I'll get with them and make a lunch to take over there today," she mused.

"I think that would be a great idea," he agreed. "I have to work the gate today, but if you need me, I can be to you in minutes."

"We will be fine," she promised him. "With Evie and Hope, I don't think anything will happen, but we will be on alert. I promise."

Lucky nodded and kissed her goodbye as he gathered his things to head into his first day of work since they'd officially mated. Sofia felt good about her idea and placed a call to Hope first, asking if she could get Evie to help her welcome Cheyenne properly into the pride.

Chapter 14

Cheyenne hovered over the toilet in the large building the Shaw pride claimed had been the old dorms for their young Guardians during their training. She'd woken from a dream about the things she'd seen at her old pride and her stomach revolted. There were too many images running through her mind to get a good night's sleep, and the bags under her eyes gave that away.

The Guardian, Malaki, had come by to speak with her the night before, explaining how they'd lost track of the wolves who'd taken over her old pride's lands. If her uncles had the gene to take over as alpha, they would've killed those wolves with no regrets, but that wasn't the case. They couldn't do anything. First of all, because of their age. Her grandfather's brothers were too old to fight, but they did try to protect everyone, at first.

If she hadn't played dead while Ellington and Hurley hid, she wouldn't be alive today. And there shouldn't be any blame placed on her uncles. They did what they had to do to stay alive, hiding Ella and Gianna until the war was over.

They'd made the decision to grab her and the remaining two females and run once they realized the destruction of the Patton pride was over.

She knew that her grandfather was in on the murder of his own pride. She'd seen him tell the wolves to kill his family first…her mother…the children of the pride.

He didn't want anyone left, but the wolves, as vicious as they were, took him out too. She didn't know what deal he'd had with the wolves, but they must've thought taking out Alan was better for everyone involved.

Was it money? Was it for the lands? She'd heard of the wolves killing prides to commandeer lands before, but there was something that wasn't right with the whole attack, and she wanted answers.

The thought caused her to vomit again. The images in her head were too vivid. No one should see so many murders in their lifetime.

The door to the bathroom opened and the two elder females from her pride rushed to her side. "Oh, honey."

Ella was there to hold her long, red hair back from her face. She heaved again; thankful nothing came out.

Lucky

Her stomach was already empty.

"Everything is going to be okay," Gianna promised.

"The nightmares are so bad," Cheyenne cried. "I try to be strong, but I just...can't."

"Everything is going to be okay," Ella said, continuing to stroke her hair. "The Shaw pride is now our pride, and they have a reputation for being one of the strongest and most understanding prides in the world. You have to trust they will care for us and keep us safe. I know I do."

"I trust them," she sighed, sitting back on her bottom, crossing her legs as she used the wall for support. "I do, but with the news that the wolves have disappeared, it scares me."

"Honey," Gianna cooed. "You are so brave. You did what you were supposed to do. There was no other option for you once they rushed the pride. We are so proud of you for trying to save the children."

Gianna stopped talking when Cheyenne lunged for the toilet, heaving again, but this time, she emptied her stomach completely. She had no idea there was anything left to purge.

"I'm going to call the healer," Ella advised, standing from her spot next to Cheyenne. "You need something to relax you and your stomach."

Thankfully, there were some human drugs that would help, and Cheyenne was sure the Shaw pride's healer would be there as soon as possible even if it was three in the morning.

Like she'd thought, the older healer, Harold, rushed into the room only five minutes later. In his hand was a black bag. She assumed it had all of his necessary tools to check over a pride member who was sick or in distress.

"I know you are not mated," he began, kneeling at her side, "but I am going to wear gloves anyway. I'd like to give you a quick physical to make sure there is nothing else going on."

"I swear it's only the nightmares, healer," she promised, removing a hair tie from her wrist to pull her messy hair up into a bun.

"Are you feeling well enough to move to your room, or would you like for me to examine you here?" He was a good male, and the entire pride had spoken highly of the healer since she'd arrived.

When she tried to move from the bathroom floor, her body revolted and she slumped down beside the toilet.

"We can do this here," he advised with a soft smile. "Let me see your arm. We will start with your blood pressure."

The healer produced a cuff from his bag and started his examination. By the time he got to her face, he'd checked her eyes and ears. "Stick out your tongue for me and say 'ahh.'"

He frowned at his findings, but before she was able to ask what the problem was, the healer had turned to Ella and Gianna. "Could you help me get her to her

Lucky

room, please?"

The two elder females helped Cheyenne to her feet, moving her across the hall. Once she was leaned up against the mound of pillows on her bed, Harold had produced a bag of fluids, "You are very dehydrated. I'm going to set up this IV and ask that you sleep until it's done. When I come back in an hour, I will check you over again, and we will go from there."

Cheyenne closed her eyes when the healer said he was giving her something in the IV for her nausea. It was strong enough to put her to sleep, and she actually let the medicine seep into her system without a fight. Any other time, she would've panicked with the presence of a drug that would help her sleep.

When she awoke, the two elder females from her pride were at her bedside, sitting in chairs. Ella and Gianna smiled warmly at her, but looked over their shoulders at someone else in the room. She was so groggy, but she didn't miss the Guardian named Malaki standing in the background.

"Cheyenne, wake up, honey," Ella cooed. "The healer is on his way to check you again."

"I'm fine, really," she mumbled and fought off the effects of the medicine. "I'm not sick."

"We know this, but we want to make sure you are at least hydrated," Ella said, looking up at the bag attached to the side of her bed. It was empty. "He's given you two bags of fluids since he saw you last. You were more dehydrated than we thought."

"Oh," she blushed. "I didn't know."

"It's hard to tell sometimes," the healer announced as he entered her room in the old dorms. "I think two bags should be enough. You are going to have to drink a lot of water for the rest of the day so I don't have to add more."

"I can do that," she promised the healer, glancing over his shoulder. The Guardian she'd met before, Malaki, was there, watching everything. The male didn't speak, and she even tested the scent in the air to see if there was some sort of connection, but she found nothing. The elders had always trained her to look for scents; even scents that indicated a male might be interested.

So, what was up with the Shaw pride's Guardian? And why was he always around her?

Cheyenne didn't know, and at the moment, she was still groggy from the medicine. She'd have to deal with those questions later…when she was back to herself.

Sofia stood at the kitchen in Lucky's cabin, making a large pot of beef stew. The temperatures had dropped again, but there was no snow in the forecast. Her mate had been helping his brother deliver wood to the other pride members for most of the afternoon once he finally left their bed.

A smile tugged at the corner of her lips. He'd been

Lucky

nothing but kind and thoughtful to her when she had a slight panic attack a few nights ago.

He'd been on her mind ever since he'd left earlier, and her panther was pushing her thoughts about him. She had never been in love, but she felt something brewing inside her...

And she was sure it was love.

They had a connection by touch, and now a cub, but the time they'd been together over the last month may have just solidified her need for a loving mate.

She sensed him before he even stepped foot on the porch. Her soft smile widened as the door opened and he kicked off his boots before he tracked in mud into the cabin. She called it *his* cabin, but she knew it was *their* cabin. The moment they'd touched, what was hers became his, and what was his became hers. It was still weird to think like that, but it was true.

"Hello, princess," he cooed as he came up behind her, wrapping his arms around her belly. His large hand rested over their cub, and she relaxed into his hold.

"Hi," she breathed.

"Whatever you're cooking smells amazing," he praised, turning her around so he could press his lips to hers. "I've been thinking, and I want to talk to you. Do we have time before dinner to sit on the couch together?"

"We do," she agreed, turning slightly to lower the temperature on the gas stove.

Lucky took her by the hand, and Sofia tried to ignore her panther's growl of approval for her mate's touch.

Once he sat her down, Lucky sighed heavily, pulling her to his chest.

"I haven't stopped thinking about you all day," he admitted.

She turned in his hold and stroked a stray blond hair from his face. "I feel the same way."

Her words were calculated, and she wanted to finally tell him how she felt. The entire day…all she thought about was Lucky…and their mating.

"I want you to know that I not only respect you because you are my mate and you're carrying my cub, but there's more, Sofia," he paused. The way he said her name sent a thrill through her bones. Her panther was just as happy about what they knew was coming next. "I know love is a weird thing for panthers, and we aren't like most humans, but the time I've spent with you over the last month has stirred feelings inside me. My panther, and I know yours probably feels the same, keeps nudging me to express what is in our minds."

"Tell me, Lucky," she urged, pulling on her old-school way of thinking.

"I swear before our gods and the alpha that I love you, Sofia," he finally admitted. "There is a connection between us that just isn't because of the touch. I know other males in the pride have gone through the same thing we've gone through, and each one of us is different…"

She reached up and placed one finger over his lips to stop him from talking. "Lucky Cooper, we were destined to be mates, and our gods made that happen. I've been going over my own thoughts today, and I know that I love you, too."

"Oh, Sofia," he breathed as he took her lips. The first press was sweet, but the second was harsher. When he pulled back, she cried out from the loss. "I promise to love you forever. My pledge is to the pride, but you will come first before them. I'd had moments in my life where I didn't think I would ever find a mate, but once my panther chose you, I knew you'd be mine forever. I may not always be the best male, but I'm going to damn well try to care for you."

"You've already proven your worth to me, Lucky Cooper," she reminded him. "There will never be a time I will doubt your protection, and I will give you the family you deserve. I honestly can say that I truly love you."

"And I love you, Sofia Corvera," he admitted, kissing her again. She felt a stirring between her legs, and although it was foreign, her body knew exactly what she needed.

It wasn't like a female to initiate sex, but Sofia was learning she was a bit different from the tales of the elders. She wanted to show him how much she loved him in all ways.

Sofia didn't release her hold on his lips as she threw her leg over his lap, pressing her body down on his hardness. They'd only had sex once, but that one time was enough to make her crave his seed. She wanted to feel him inside her.

"Make love to me, Lucky," she urged, grinding her body against his. "I need you."

"Say no more, my mate," he growled, using his panther claws to shred her pajama pants. They were nothing but scraps of material by the time he exposed her wetness to his hand.

The moment his cock breached her body, she hummed low in her throat, and her panther snarled. "Oh, gods…"

"Take what you need from me," he urged as she rode him.

Lucky was giving her control, and even though she knew absolutely nothing about sex, she let her body and panther take the lead, moving up and down until she found a rhythm that made both of them moan in pleasure.

His hand snaked between their bodies, flipping it over so he could use his thumb to rub against the tiny nub between her legs. The action sent her body into a sense of pleasure she'd only had once, and that was when his canines sank into her skin, marking her as his mate once more.

"Your body wants to orgasm, Sofia," he advised, making her blush. His filthy words were almost embarrassing, but she was so lost in the pleasure, she didn't respond. "Let go, princess. Let the sensations take over."

And with his words, she focused on the feeling.

Lucky

There was a build up this time. It was nothing like the immediate climax she'd had on their first night together. No, this was different.

"I want...more...more of you," she begged, focusing on her body. It wanted his cock deep inside her, ramming her body until her climax was over. The desires she felt with him were nothing like she'd ever imagined.

She whimpered once, and Lucky gave her what she wanted. Sofia called out his name as they came together, fast...frantic...hard.

"Shhh," he cooed against her ear. "Relax against me. I will be here until you catch your breath."

Chapter 15

*L*ucky *reluctantly left Sofia at* her brother's home with Mary Grace. The Guardians were assembling a search party one last time to find the wolves. They would be going back to the Patton's old lands to see if the murderous wolves had returned.

"If there has been no sign of their return, I want you to return to the pride immediately," Talon ordered. "We can't protect lands that do not belong to us."

Talon had been working with the sheriff on the reasoning behind the Patton pride's inability to pay their mortgage. They'd found some information, but as with all shifters, nothing was concrete. They'd stayed in hiding for thousands of years, and a pride wouldn't have their information out in the open for anyone to access.

"I will be there with you," Garrett spoke up, coming

to Talon's side. "I haven't had any more visions since the first, but that doesn't mean the danger has passed."

"Do we even know the name of the wolves who murdered the pride?" Kraven asked.

"No," Garrett growled. "After an extensive records search, it looked as if the pride wasn't making the money they needed to pay for their lands. Most of the pride members were getting too old to hold jobs, and with the current state of the country, they couldn't find jobs. All we know is that this pack of wolves had keys to the cabins, and they'd been in the area up to ten days before the attack. I'm led to believe that Alan Patton was working a deal with the wolves. If they've run off, it means that deal was never completed."

"Do you think the wolves found out about the land being foreclosed on?" Lucky stepped forward. "If that's the case, maybe the killings were an act of revenge for Alan's betrayal."

"That's what I'm thinking," Garrett agreed, turning toward Talon. "If you are ready, I have some weapons to distribute, and we can be on our way."

"Be safe, and keep me posted," Talon ordered as he nodded, then the crowd of Guardians left the office.

Only the Protectors and a handful of Guardians would remain on the lands to protect the pride while the others drove to the small town just west of Nashville to investigate. Garrett had expressed his concern earlier because the Shaw pride was the closest one, but Talon assured him that his Guardians would be okay that far away from him for the short amount of time it took to get there and back. Lucky knew he could still call out for Talon if he needed the alpha's strength for any reason. He wasn't worried.

However, he was worried about being away from his mate for the next seven or eight hours. Just knowing he would be that far away from Sofia set him on edge, but he tried to not let it show. If he showed any sign of being feral without his new mate, Talon would've ordered him to stay back.

Lucky had his own reasons why he wanted to join in on the group going to the pride. He wanted to find the son of a bitch who had run his pregnant mate off the road, and he sure as fuck wanted to know why they'd come here to harm one of their pride.

The moment he stepped off the front porch of the alpha's home, his eyes landed on who he believed was the reason…Cheyenne.

The young, red-haired female stood with the two elder females, Ella and Gianna. The three of them appeared strong, but the flashes of amber sparks in their eyes told a different story. They were scared and angry, and he didn't blame them.

As his eyes moved from the females, he caught Malaki standing next to one of the trucks they were going to use, and his eyes were locked on the female. Lucky's eyebrow shot up as he watched Malaki's eyes darken for a second before Winter interrupted him and handed him a set of keys.

Savage cranked up the dark grey truck that belonged to the pride and rolled his window down, "You riding with me?"

"Yeah," Lucky said, turning one last time to glance up the road to where Savage's home sat, seeing as all of the lights were off except the one by the front door. He prayed his mate was sleeping well, and he prayed no harm came to his pride while he and the others were away.

The drive to the small town of Greenbriar, Tennessee took just over three hours, and when they arrived, Lucky and Savage followed Kraven's truck to a spot he and Malaki had used before to spy on the wolves. They got into place and killed the engines, casting them in total darkness. It was barely after eleven at night, but they didn't need light to see. Half of the Guardians shifted, and Lucky was one of them to pull forth his panther. If he found the male who'd harmed his mate, he wanted his panther present so they could avenge her.

The panther's breath came out in a cloud with each exhale. The animal was scenting the air, hoping each time he'd scent a wolf nearby. It was disappointed only a few times before the stench of their natural enemy reached his nose. Lucky's panther wasn't the only one to scent the wolves, either.

Their mission was to bring justice to the wolves, and with Winter Blue as Talon's second-in-command, they rushed the home that had belonged to the Patton pride.

The main house was close to the property's edge

Lucky

where the Guardians were hiding. One leap over the flimsy fence got Lucky close to the one-story, ranch-style home with weathered wooden siding.

The moment they surrounded the home, a howl sounded inside, and that was when all hell broke loose.

Wolves and males darted from every door and window. They ran headfirst into the gathering panthers, but they didn't fight. No, they stopped, digging their nails into the ground before turning and scurrying away, running for the back of the pride's land and forest.

The Guardians gave chase, and Savage was the first one to catch a wolf, ending his life with one bite to its throat, leaving it on the ground. Winter, in human form, let out a vicious curse, sending Lucky's panther in the direction of the older Guardian. When he found him, he was bleeding from his fighting hand, and there was a half-shifted male coming at him with a knife.

The panther pounced on the male, knocking away the knife, giving Winter a chance to shift for protection and healing. It didn't take more than a few seconds before they both were on the male, ending his life just as Savage had done the other wolf.

Howls, yips, and human screams were heard all throughout the land. Lucky and Winter rushed to the closest sound, seeing Kraven winning a fight with a dirty-looking male who was about the same size.

They turned again, seeing men and wolves fleeing back toward the main house. They had a good head start on Lucky, but he was one of the fastest males in the

Shaw pride. He would make sure each of them paid for what they'd done.

By the time he reached the first male, the other three were already inside a blue truck...the same blue truck that had rammed his mate. He could see the paint on the dent in the fender, and that made his panther roar.

He slashed his claws against the first male's gut, spilling his insides as he screamed for mercy, but Lucky and his panther had no time to finish him off. He could suffer while he bled out on the ground of the children he'd killed not long ago.

The car lunged forward, trying to hit the panther, but Lucky was faster, using his hind legs to jump onto the hood of the car. When the three males noticed he wasn't going to stop coming for them, the one driving pulled out a gun and held it out the window, firing two shots.

Both of them missed the panther.

However, when the car spun around, his claws had no purchase on the shiny paint. Lucky's panther rolled off the hood and onto the ground, snarling as he felt horrendous pain in his shoulder. Standing up was no option. Every single time he tried to put weight on it, his right side would crumble beneath him.

Other Guardians rushed to the area, but none of them were able to stop the vehicle. Garrett flashed into the driveway, looked around, and flashed out. It was only seconds later that they heard the vehicle crash a few blocks away.

"That sheriff might be good for something after all,"

Lucky

Winter mumbled, still bleeding from his wounds.

The panthers ran down the road, finding the car stuck headfirst into a tree. The wolves were running, and Lucky and his Guardian brothers gave chase.

The woods were a bit different than what he was used to at home, but it didn't stop him from jumping over downed trees, looking for any animal paths through the forest. The wolves were good. They knew their way around, and it was causing a disadvantage for the panthers.

The more they chased, the further away the wolves got, and he heard his brothers roar in the darkness. It didn't take long until the woods were silent and the only sound was the panting from the panthers in his own pride.

"We lost them," Savage cursed, slamming his hand against a small tree, knocking it over on its side.

"It's not over yet," Winter advised as he scanned the area. "Everyone, split up and search for scents. Call out to Talon if you find them. Otherwise, meet back here in the next half hour."

Lucky had his own mission. He wanted the blood of the wolves who'd come for his mate. He had a feeling they didn't know it was Sofia they'd harmed. He had a feeling it was Cheyenne they wanted, and then he wanted to know what was so special about Patton's granddaughter that caused an entire pack of wolves to come hunting for her on the Shaw's land.

Sofia cried out as the trucks arrived around nine in the morning. Lucky was the first one out, and she ran into his arms. He scented of their mating, and she relaxed into his hold.

"I was so worried," she mumbled into his chest.

"I'm fine. We are all fine," he promised, kissing her head. "Oh, my love. We are all okay, but the wolves escaped."

"No," she cried. "No!"

"Shhh," he cooed. "Let me take you home, and after I have a meeting with Talon, I will explain soon." He pushed her back slightly, using his thumbs to wipe away her tears. "I promise you that you are safe. I won't let anything happen to you."

"You promise to tell me everything, right?" she pushed.

"With my life," he vowed, kissing her again. "I have to see our alpha."

"Hurry home," she begged and released him, but she was reluctant, holding his shirt for a moment longer.

"Go to the cabin and wait for me," he said as the other Guardians arrived, waiting for him to follow them inside.

Sofia was worried, and her heart was on edge. As she looked around at the Guardians who'd come home with her mate, she noticed they were in different stages of healing. The worst was Winter Blue. His arms were covered in blood and the remnants of old claw marks from what she already knew were the wolf's claws.

A cry sounded from the front steps of the alpha's home. Nova, Winter's mate, ran with all of her might, slamming into the father of her cubs. She worried over him as the males tried to assure their mates they were unharmed.

"Sofia," Lucky called out. "Go to our cabin and get it warm for us, please. I will be there after I debrief the alpha."

"Uh huh, okay," she said on autopilot.

The walk back to Lucky's cabin was lonely and cold, and none of the other pride came out to check on them. It was eerie to see how desolate the pride was, and that was saying something. She never remembered a time when the pride didn't welcome home the Guardians after a mission to stop a group from coming to hurt them.

A bubble of anger rose up in her throat, wondering why they were so quiet. The initial fight was to protect the new pride members, and there was no one there to support them.

No one.

None.

"Sofia!" a voice called as she pressed her fist to her heart.

When she turned around, Malaki was there, his hands out in front of him like he was going to catch her.

"Mal, don't," she cried.

"I know what you're thinking, and I want you to

know that Talon has ordered the pride to take refuge in their homes until we figure out where they're hiding and what the hell is going on."

"I'm scared, Mal," she said, giving in to her fears, telling her best friend instead of her mate. Malaki stopped, turning toward her.

"Sofia, you know that I love you, right?" he asked, but didn't touch her.

"I do," she nodded.

"Lucky is your destined mate, and he should be the one to reassure you of what's going to happen if those wolves come back," he pressed, looking over his shoulder. There were no other Guardians around.

"I also have to go meet with Talon, but I wanted to catch you for a moment to tell you that I approve of Lucky. He will protect you and love you for the rest of your lives. Don't worry about me anymore. I think I am finally understanding my new life. It took a while, but…I'm going to be okay."

"Are you? Really?" she asked, stepping forward. God, she loved her friend, but nothing like she felt for Lucky.

"Go, love your mate, and tell him every single day that you love him, Sofia," Malaki finalized, turning on his heal.

"I will," she whispered to him, but he was too far away to hear her.

By the time she reached their cabin, the air was cold, and she shivered as she added another log to the fire. The

Lucky

soft, blue blanket she found on the back of the couch was just enough to have her body heat warm her until the cabin caught up. The temperatures were already below freezing, but with the arrival of her mate, she hadn't noticed the cold until she was alone.

The front door opened and Lucky came in, stopping at the threshold. They stared at each other for the longest time, and he never shut the door, letting the cold air inside his cabin.

"Sofia," he breathed, his eyes sparking amber.

"Yes, Lucky," she replied, feeling his mating connection deep in her chest.

"Before we talk about anything else, I just want you to know something," he said, then paused.

"What is it?" she asked, not wanting to wait for an answer.

"God damnit, Sofia Corvera," he breathed, slamming the door. Her mate marched across the room and took her into her arms. "I know our species isn't made like humans, and I know that we've only been mates for a few weeks, but I fucking love you. I love you more than I ever thought I'd love another being in my entire life."

"Oh, Lucky," she gasped, tears building in her eyes. She'd waited for this moment her entire adult life. It'd take a lot of other females longer to find their true mates, but the gods had gifted her with a mate right from her own pride. "I love you, too."

"We may not have had the traditional courting that

other males have had with their mates, but…I know…I *feel* it to my core. We still have a lot to learn about each other, and I heard what Malaki said to you earlier. I know for sure that you do love me even though you have a strong friendship bond with him."

"Please don't hate him for loving me," she begged, grasping his plaid shirt. "He is my friend."

"I know that now," he nodded. "I also know that you are mine…forever."

The End…

Note From the Author (That's ME!)

Thank you all for being patient while I worked through my medical issues and got myself back into shape to write more of the pride.

2021 can go fly a kite. Ugh.

I know we've all had a weird year and a half, and I hope this story made you smile. Lucky and Sofia have always been on my list of "Instalove" ideas.

I hope you fell in love with them while Malaki was finding his way in this world.

You know his story will be next.

Hold on to your hats, I have a feeling it's going to be a crazy one.

~Theresa

Other Books by Theresa Hissong:

Fatal Cross Live!
Fatal Desires
Fatal Temptations
Fatal Seduction

Rise of the Pride:
Talon
Winter
Savage
The Birth of an Alpha
Ranger
Kye
The Healer
Dane
Booth

Morgan Clan Bears
Mating Season
Mating Instinct

Incubus Tamed
Thirst

Standalone Novella
Something Wicked

Book for Charity:
Fully Loaded

<u>Club Phoenix</u>
The Huntress

<u>Cycle of Sin on Tour</u>
Rocked (A Rockstar Reverse Harem Novel)

About Theresa Hissong:

Theresa Hissong is a USA Today Bestselling author. She writes paranormal romance, rockstar romance, and romantic suspense.
She enjoys spending her days and nights creating the perfect love affair, and she takes those ideas to paper. When she's not writing, Theresa spends her free time traveling and attending concerts all over the United States.
Look for other exciting reads…coming very soon!